IN THE

BEAST'S

CAGE

MAC ALTGELT

The Book Guild Ltd

First published in Great Britain in 2021 by
The Book Guild Ltd
9 Priory Business Park
Wistow Road, Kibworth
Leicestershire, LE8 0RX
Freephone: 0800 999 2982
www.bookguild.co.uk
Email: info@bookguild.co.uk
Twitter: @bookguild

Typeset in 11pt Adobe Garamond Pro

Printed and bound by CPI Group (UK) Ltd, Croydon, CR0 4YY

ISBN 978 1913551 926

British Library Cataloguing in Publication Data.
A catalogue record for this book is available from the British Library.

For my family,
Alejandra, Sophia, & Otto,
without whom nothing is possible

And my parents,
Ernie & Susan,
From whom my love of books was born

In Memoriam:
Beloved Aunts, Margy & Susie
My best friend, Willis

-PROLOGUE-

THE JUNGLE'S RESENTMENT HAD ALWAYS BEEN SOMETHING tangible for him. Since his first day on the job he had sensed its hatred, its yearning to be rid of them. Today had been yet another stark reminder of that terrible reality. Of that eternal struggle between man and the natural world they sought to exploit. The jungle was a breathing, living entity in symbiosis with the countless species that constituted its whole, and they were the cancer that threatened it. They carved new veins through which their disease spread, infecting deeper into the ancient body that had known such robust health prior to its initial exposure. Before patient zero.

He attempted to mop the sweat and blood from his brow with an overly saturated bandana but succeeded only in smearing it around his face. He conjured saliva from the depths of his throat and spat on the ground with disgust, cursing under his breath. They were starting to load the bodies up now.

It was about time, he thought. *Pretty soon they'll start to putrefy and stink. Corpses don't hold together long in this humidity.*

He replayed the events of the day in his head over and over again, wondering, as he always did, how it was that he had come to be in such a lamentable place.

The day had started normally enough. He'd arisen with as much peace of mind as could be expected from one forced to toil illegally two thousand miles away from their home, and gone over his itinerary with calmness. It was pretty standard and contained nothing within it overtly alarming. These days most of the game-trapping was handled by the indigenous peoples, who could be exploited as much for their intimate knowledge of the rainforest as for their willingness to work for almost no pay. Today he was to accompany them while checking their traps and he was hopeful, as the night had been clear and moonlit, which always meant an increase in the nocturnal movements of the jungle's varied creatures.

Since he was still relatively new to the trade, his assignments had mainly consisted up to this point of high-yield, low-dollar stuff like bird-catching. Birds could be caught in bulk and, since most of them were captured only to be killed for their feathers, skins or other body parts, it didn't matter if they were injured due to the inexperience of the trafficker. There were exceptions to this, of course. Toucans and scarlet macaws were certainly high-dollar items that required a certain degree of care. If, as the collateral damage of his own carelessness, he showed up with a bunch of stiffening macaw carcasses sprinkled throughout his night's haul, he'd have hell to pay and he knew it. Still, this was mainly the responsibility of the indigenes employed in the capture of these animals in the first place, so he wasn't too worried. The only part of these rookie assignments that really got to him was the lack of money involved for himself. It perhaps goes without saying that one only finds one's self in such a pitiable position when one has no other alternative and, more often than not, it is a problem that can only be solved by money, which must first be obtained before it can deliver one out of bondage.

He sipped a cup of good coffee gone bad and thought through the day's work ahead of him. He hoped that the favourable conditions of the previous night might lead to some unexpected and more profitable yields. After all, even when targeting birds, he was always careful to have the ground traps set just in case. If he turned up later in the day with a jaguar in tow, his superiors weren't likely to turn him away because his catch fell slightly outside the scope of his original assignment. In fact, during the course of his brief employment he had enjoyed a certain degree of prosperity that had been realised in just this way. At various intervals of his fledgling career as a trafficker, he had been successful in procuring a variety of these "accidental", and yet enormously fortuitous, captures. These included a highly valuable black caiman, two anacondas, several howler monkeys, even more spider monkeys, countless macaws and just a few toucans. Now he had his eye set on a jaguar, which he felt would round out his portfolio nicely and provide him with the ammunition he desperately needed in order to seek more lucrative contracts going forward. He hoped, perhaps a bit naively, that he might finally prove himself by means of this crown jewel of the trade.

He finished the rotten coffee, nearly gagging on the grounds that comprised the bulk of his final sip, and tossed the tin mug back into his tent as if it had been to blame for the unpalatable dregs. He stepped out into the dense air, yesterday's sweat still beaded and pearly as if fresh on the surface of his muck-smeared skin. He fielded a few casual greetings without feeling from the other members of the camp, then made a beeline for his ATV. His excitement to check the traps was mounting and he wasn't eager to get held up any longer by early-morning platitudes. He kneeled as if in prayer at the side of his ATV and checked the engine casing for snakes. Necessity demanded that he perform this ritual each morning before mounting his ride, because the cold blood of the reptiles meant that the motor's warmth attracted them, and the result was that they could often be found nesting lazily amongst the twists of metal that still radiated with the latent heat of the previous day's use. Were he to fail in this, a bite from some envenomed creature, startled abruptly to waking by the explosive vibrations of a quiet engine stirred unexpectedly back to life, could very easily place him in a life-threatening situation, being as they were very far from the closest stock of anti-venom, or medical attention in general. This, of course, was only one of many such daily customs that helped to fill out a lengthy checklist of similar occupations, such as checking his shoes for wandering spiders each morning before jamming his feet in. The Amazon, as they all learned very early on and in different ways, was as full of creatures that could kill you as ones that could make you rich, and the former was something he felt strongly compelled to avoid.

After checking that the engine was clear of deadly snakes, and that the tank was full, he ascended to his mount and sped off in the direction of the indigenous village that was home to his local trapping counterparts. He knew the trail well and it did not take him long to arrive. When he pulled, up his men were already waiting for him. As soon as they noticed his approach, they moved to intercept the ATV, greeting its rider with the excitement of a first time, as they did every time. In spite of how long they had been working together, many months at this point, the novelty of the white man and the ATV never failed to overwhelm them whenever he appeared in their village. They marvelled at him as he dismounted, rolling his eyes at the childlike wonder that he simply could not reconcile with the dark nature of their relationship. The purity and innocence of their savage revelry never failed to resurrect the conscience that he had spent months silencing within himself, and it always left a disagreeable taste in his mouth.

He waved down their excited exclamations and, employing a well-understood hand gesture, indicated that they should proceed directly to the traps. It was by means of a series of these hand and body signs, unique to them alone, that the language barrier that had existed between them at the inception of their partnership had ultimately been triumphed over. Calling again to his aid this distinctive language that had him often gesticulating wildly like a lunatic, he succeeded quickly in wrangling his team. Together the group continued on foot into the brush.

After a half hour of laboured hiking and profuse sweating, they arrived at the first trap. This was one of his surreptitious ground traps and, to his great disappointment, it seemed the trap had been triggered but had failed to fully enclose whatever had tripped the gate. The cage was empty and mocking. It was a significant blow since clear nights in the rainforest were few and far between, and it was impossible to speculate as to when the next might occur.

He took the blow in stride, however, and indicated that the trap should be reset and rebaited. The operation took only a few minutes and they were back on the trail shortly thereafter in pursuit of better results.

Though his assignment had been more bird-trapping, his anxiety regarding the potentially more lucrative ground traps, given the favourable conditions of the previous evening, meant that he led his men to these first. He knew the bird traps would be full, they always were, and there was no good reason to give them priority over something that had the possibility of being many times more valuable, especially when that value was in increasing jeopardy with each passing moment during which the animal was not properly sedated. Were a trapped animal to injure itself inside the cage because it had been left for too great a duration and become frantic, it might become unsellable. If it were to become mortally wounded, permanently disabled or mutilate its own coat with flesh wounds, its ultimate black-market value would undoubtedly respond negatively in kind, potentially all the way down to zero. With this thought plaguing the back of his mind, he hastened his steps towards the next trap.

The grass was tall on either side of the trail as the group neared the second trap. Though it was still a good hundred yards off and completely obscured by the tall grass, every man knew without a doubt that the trap was full and that it was something big that had been caught. They heard the tell-tale heavy padded steps, and the agitated, guttural snarl that could not be mistaken. It was the crown jewel: the jaguar. The men stopped in astonishment and listened, breathing heavily. The jaguar's sound began to fade into oblivion as his ears filled with the pounding of his own heart and the sound of blood coursing through his veins. His breath was like fire and he reached out involuntarily to steady himself on a tree that was not there. The towering grass gave way under his touch and he nearly lost his balance. Regaining his self-control, he pulled the pack from his back and began to search through it. After a few moments spent rummaging, he extracted what looked like a pistol, but oddly elongated and with an enormously fat barrel. Examining it, he continued hunting through the pack with his free hand until he produced a small black case. From the case he drew a large, metal dart that resembled a kind of flighted syringe and was full to bursting of some mysterious liquid, the true purpose of which was well known to all present. He loaded the dart into the gun, indicated with a sign that his men should wait where they were, and proceeded alone through the tall grass towards the source of the jaguar's flustered calls.

He approached with caution, listening closely. It was probable that he had nothing to fear, since jaguars were typically solitary creatures. However, if this one was still young enough, it was possible that an enraged mother might be close by, and he knew well that any resulting encounter would very likely end in the triumph of the mother over himself.

He reached the edge of the clearing in which the trap was set, barely daring to breathe, and, parting the curtain of grass, peered through to the cage. It was there! A large male jaguar, several years of age and clearly beyond the period of life during which it would have been dependent on its mother. He let out a gasp and a laugh simultaneously, slapping his knee and setting a nearby group of birds to startled flight. He approached the cage casually, drinking in his victory. To his delight, the animal seemed in perfect health and completely unscathed by any injury, either recent or in its deeper past. Worrying that his presence might alarm the beast, however, he quickly raised his gun and fired. The effect was immediate. The great cat let out an extraordinary roar as the dart pierced its shoulder, then rushed at the cage towards its captor. Hitting the barrier, it spun, its rage turning instantly to confusion. Gradually, the confusion morphed into languor and the jaguar dropped to its belly, licking its chops. After a few more brief moments, during which it was clear that the animal was fighting a desperate battle against the effect of the powerful tranquiliser, it appeared to give up the struggle and became quite calm. At last, defeated, the mighty king of the rainforest lowered its beautiful head to the earth and slept profoundly.

The indigenous trappers had followed their orders precisely and were waiting exactly where they had been left when he returned to them beaming. He confirmed the success of their enterprise with a casual gesture and then further indicated that it was time to return to the village. Now that the jaguar had been sedated and could be left without any fear of self-mutilation, he needed to return to his own camp so that he could get a flatbed truck with which to transport the sleeping animal. He had decided with only a small pang of conscience not to bother with the other traps that still remained unchecked, knowing that his arrival with a jaguar would grant him the immediate forgiveness of his employers, not to mention their immense gratitude. Enlivened by the extraordinary success of the morning, the group set out for home at a trot, laughing together in spite of their different tongues and giving each other high fives, which were a favourite thing of the indigenes ever since he had taught them what they were in the early days of their partnership.

They made it back to the village in just over half the time it had taken them to reach the jaguar trap earlier that morning. With a flick of the hand that was a testament to his fluency in their covert language, he informed his men that they were not to tell anyone about the jaguar until he returned. Mounting again his ATV without bothering to check for snakes, he rode off towards his camp at a speed that bordered crazy, with maybe just a toe over the line. When he neared the camp, he slowed to a more reasonable speed, careful not to appear too overexcited in the company of his brother traffickers and risk them getting wise to the great triumph that was to be his alone. When asked why he needed a flatbed he made up some excuse about an injured indigene in need of transport, a fairly common occurrence, and this seemed to satisfy the overseer of their meagre camp motor pool. He examined the bed of the beaten and rusting truck, checking first the integrity of the hoist and then the functionality of the wench's engine. After satisfying himself that both were in perfect working order in spite of their appearance, he climbed into the cab and made his way back towards the village.

It took him longer in the truck than it had on the ATV, being forced now to follow the roads instead of the narrower trails, but he made good time and arrived back in the indigenous camp before noon. He found his men right where he had left them and signalled for two to ride on back and the last, whom he considered to be his lead man, to join him in the cab. They did so with perfect understanding and obedience, apparently as excited as he was and heart-breakingly unaware of just how badly they were being taken advantage of. Very little of this jaguar's value would find its way into their pockets, and he felt his conscience fire up inside himself again as the thought passed over his mind.

Clearing his throat without any need to, he pushed the unwelcome benevolence back into the abyss of his own heart and cranked the engine. Again, it took longer to reach the trap than it had on foot and for the same reason. They had to drive completely around the clearing to where they knew the ground was hard enough to support the weight of the truck and then into the tall grass, through which they had already passed by foot earlier that morning.

It was mid-afternoon when they arrived back at the trap and they were pleased to see that the tranquiliser was still doing its job.

The jaguar was broadside on the ground, deep in the throes of a drug-induced sleep, from which it would undoubtedly wake very soon. He loaded up another dart in anticipation of needing it and began to unwind the wench's cable so that the trap could be lifted in its entirety onto the bed of the truck. As the cable unwound itself from the spool, he swivelled the hoist to a position directly above the cage. The whole operation didn't take long since very little slack was needed in order to fix the wench's hook to the roof of the cage. In another five minutes the trap was sitting safely atop the flatbed with the jaguar dozing away peacefully unaware inside of it.

He turned to his men smiling, the triumph of the day written across every premature crease of his face. Next to him his lead man beamed back. The other men, however, did not return their smiles. His mouth flattened into a grimace as he tried to read their expressions and understand the cause of their abnormal behaviour, so out of keeping with the jovial mood of their party up to that point. For their part, they did not see their captain, as their combined focus went out past him and towards the grass-line. As he turned to follow their gaze, his vision turned suddenly to a sheet of violent red. Only after did he hear the crack of the gunshot. He wiped the blood splatter from his eyes just in time to see his lead man keel over at his side, the smile of their collective victory still etched across his unknowing face.

The initial crack was followed closely by others, but his surprise had temporarily paralysed him and he was rooted to his spot. The two other indigenes, apparently not as afflicted, fled in opposite directions, and he watched the ground behind them dance as they drew the fire towards themselves. Seizing this fleeting opportunity, he conjured back his reason from the abyss and made a break for the tall grass. He knew this manoeuvre had been spotted when he heard the bullets whizzing past his ears, but he never looked back. When he reached the safety of the grass, he ran quickly along its circumference to a spot far from that where he had entered. Posting himself there and concentrating all his efforts on remaining motionless and silent, he watched as the scene continued to unfold out in the clearing in front of him. The two living indigenes had not been as lucky as he had and were now being lead towards the flatbed at the end of a rifle. One had been injured by a gunshot to the leg during their flight and struggled now to make the journey back to the clearing's centre. They were made to kneel as another large truck, up to this point entirely obscured, emerged from the grass and stopped, idling, at their side. Several more men climbed down from the cabin and he counted a total of seven from his hiding spot in the grass. He recognised them immediately as drug runners and knew that to approach would be suicide.

The illegal trades of animal trafficking and drug running in the Amazon were quite often complements of each other. The one provided services as needed for the other, and vice versa. It was not uncommon that animal carcasses would be stuffed with drugs and shipped around the world. Nothing threw off a dog's nose quite like decay and therefore the relationship was often to each party's mutual benefit. The traffickers provided the conduit through which a product could be moved, and the drug smuggler provided the muscle out here in the unforgiving jungle. It was also typically the drug guys who had bribed the right government officials in the right places, and the traffickers enjoyed the benefits of those arrangements solely as a by-product of proximity. Still, territories in the Amazon were mostly respected. An attack like this could only mean that a rival gang was seeking to extend the reach of their own operation within the basin. A cartel at war is a violent and dangerous thing, and he knew that leaving his refuge meant his life.

He was right to think so. After only a few minutes of unsuccessful communication attempts with the indigenes, each was dispatched with terrible efficiency by means of a single bullet to the head. He closed his eyes when this happened and lamented the trap that was never supposed to have been set in the first place. He watched as the drug runners turned their attention next to the cage. The cartel chiefs had always expressed an interest in exotic beasts with which to adorn their mansions, and this fact was not lost on their lower-level guys out in the field. These were his peers within their own industry, and the jaguar had as much value in its novelty for them as it did for him.

He concentrated as he tried to piece together the scene playing out in mute before his eyes. They were shaking the cage and, when the jaguar did not stir, they unlatched the gate. He figured that they must have believed that the animal had died, otherwise who would enter the cage of a captured jaguar? They did this without incident, however, even neglecting to relatch the gate behind themselves when they emerged again from the trap. He noticed this oversight and glanced over at the dart gun he had dropped far out in the depths of the clearing.

The next moments passed in confused gesticulations and a lot of pointing at the cage, which he knew meant that they were arguing over what to do with the presumed dead cat. He watched the jaguar eagerly for signs of life and found them increasingly as the moments passed. Fortunately, the runners' argument amongst themselves had escalated to a point where they no longer had any mind for anything else. In the meantime, the big cat stirred and dreamed of vengeance.

When the beast finally did return to waking life, it happened in a flash. The jaguar stood, struggling to keep its balance as the drug's effect still tugged on its nervous system, and made a break towards the open gate. The smugglers' argument was approaching maximum stride as this was occurring, and they still suspected nothing when the jaguar made its first confused leap towards them. Despite the cat's instability, it found its mark and the first man went down effortlessly. The jaguar, unlike some of the other large cats, always killed with a grace and majesty that was often quite difficult to reconcile with the reality of being attacked. As a result, the perilous situation in which the runners now found themselves was not immediately evident to them.

As each second passed, the big cat found ways to compensate for the effect of the dissipating drug, and soon it was as sturdy on its feet as it had been going into the cage on the previous night. It found another mark and pounced, closing its jaws on the man's throat in an act of savage beauty unique to its species alone. By this time, the remaining men had each recovered a small fraction of their senses and picked up their weapons, firing erratically in all directions. He hid in his grass refuge, terror re-entering his body as the wild shots threatened his safety anew. The runners, however, hit neither him nor the cat.

The jaguar continued its rampage, entirely unafflicted now and even more unafraid. It took down a third man, and then a fourth. Two of the runners, having finally regained their senses in full, climbed back into the cabin of their truck. The last, however, had considered nothing but the cat since the ordeal had first begun, believing his only hope for survival lay in confronting the beast head on. He shouldered his rifle as the cat stalked him. Sensing the danger, the jaguar made a final leap just as the rifle discharged. The two bodies met in mid-air, joined together for the briefest moment, and then crumpled lifeless to the ground in unison. There they remained connected, each having been the end of the other, vowing now in death to never part.

Seeing that their last comrade had fallen, the two surviving runners reversed their truck and disappeared as quickly as they could back into the tall grass. Back through the same opening that had served as their initial point of entry into that cursed and deadly clearing earlier that afternoon. A clearing made sepulchre to five of their brothers and three children of the Amazon.

He watched in utter dismay as the scene concluded itself. When the truck had finally gone and he could no longer hear its engine in the distance, he emerged from the grass and surveyed the carnage, thinking to himself.

These bodies will have to be taken back to the village. If not, the indigenes could cause problems.

He approached the flatbed and lifted the CB receiver from its cradle in order to call for aid. Before he pressed the button, he thought: *What if Mom could see you now? You're a long way from Georgia.*

-PART ONE-

- I -

THE DAY WAS MILD AND GREY BUT STILL SHOWING NO SIGNS of rain when Virginia Harrison emerged from her front door at 8:15 in the morning. Though it was not cold, the considerable humidity present in the air drew thick wafts of steam from the hot coffee mug in her right hand. She bent down for the paper and laughed to herself, recollecting a conversation with a friend during which her love for actual *paper* newspapers had been heavily criticised. She turned, content, robed and chuckling, and headed back inside to absorb the day's news alongside the morning's requisite caffeine. For the past five years Virginia had greeted the day exactly thus.

Anyone watching this scene unfold would have seen a pretty woman, probably in her late twenties, with smiling eyes and shoulder-length, brunette hair that fell in waves, flanking her slender, beautiful face on either side. Her eyes were brown, but so light a shade and so vibrant that one may well have sworn that they were gold. She was thin, but athletic, and her body had a grace that seemed to make each individual movement continuous and liquid. Her steps were more of a glide and the kind aura of her laughing face radiated involuntarily outward in all directions.

3

This gave her an immediate power of attraction over those whom she encountered. Such was the force of this power, that one could be excused in declaring her to be born of the same race as ancient Greece's mythical sirens; though, having met her, one would be assured she in no way shared their dark motive. In short, people liked her. Loved her, in truth. She emanated kindness and happiness, those most beneficial and contagious aspects of disposition. Meeting her inspired the shy to find their voices, the wicked to find their hearts and the complacent to rise to their potential. Furthermore, she lived in complete ignorance of this effect she produced on those around her, lending an authenticity to her actions that was easily perceived and appreciated by others, and placing her in even higher regard with all of whom she was acquainted. It would seem apparent then, that Virginia Harrison was indeed a rare creature.

It was nearly 9:30 when, energised by coffee and a good mood, Virginia appeared again at her front door, this time to face for good what the day would bring. She ran through the morning's itinerary in her head without thinking, sorting it into its most efficient order as she approached the walk. She waved involuntarily to a neighbour and gave him a smile.

The neighbour, used to this daily greeting, returned both the smile and wave, then added a hearty, "Good morning!" to his salutation.

Virginia plunged on, reaching the sidewalk at maximum stride. Her first stop of the morning was at her father's house. Always logical and stoic, the old man had recently and unexpectedly taken up some new and peculiar interests. Virginia, trying not to over-worry, had consoled herself by attributing this change merely to his advancing years, and had even found that, when he had informed her that he wished to discuss one of them with her the previous week, she was actually quite eager to hear him out.

The truth was that while, at least out loud, she blamed his age for his developing eccentricities, her heart never truly accepted her reasoning. In fact, to Virginia her father looked very much the same as he had throughout her youth. Others thought so too. Those who knew him often incorporated a jesting request for his secret to perpetual youth into their conversations with him. He had the same jet-black hair as always and eyes so dark they nearly matched. He was strong and glowing and possessed none of the weaknesses of body that one might expect in a person of his age. He was thin, but not gaunt. Tall, but not outlandish. His teeth were white and long, and his body radiated health and vitality. For these reasons and others, Virginia knew inwardly that her father's mind was as strong as ever and that his new interests were likely just the next evolution in a long life that sought for something new. Strange, perhaps, but harmless all the same.

It didn't take long for Virginia to arrive at her father's house, and she found herself approaching the front door before the clock had struck ten. It was a large house and superbly kept. She rapped on the enormous wooden door, with its bulky, bronze knocker, and waited as she heard faint sounds of movement emanate from within. A few moments later the great door swung on its hinges, revealing the statuesque figure of her father.

"Hello, sweetheart!" said the man, stooping to greet his daughter with a kiss.

"Hi, Daddy!" was the young girl's sole reply.

"Come on in. I've got some news to share and then I want your opinion on some things."

His daughter obeyed and entered the house, curiously surveying the area around her for some clue as to what might have brought her there that morning. However, much to her chagrin, the atrium looked very much as it always had, and offered no answers to the questions swimming through her mind.

The pair walked on to the inside rooms of the house in silence. It appeared the old man was in no particular rush to divulge his motive in calling this meeting, and so Virginia followed him without asking questions. They continued until her father veered left into what Virginia knew to be the old man's study. She followed. Inside the room, she was greeted by a scene completely foreign to that which she had expected. On the walls, and in place of the English hunting scenes so familiar to her, were what appeared to be anatomical depictions of all manner of beasts, scientific-looking and yellowed with age and overuse. There were so many that there was hardly any bare wall left between the ceilings and the tops of the vast bookshelves. The bookshelves too had undergone a substantial renovation since she'd last been there. The familiar volumes that had populated the shelves of her youth (classic fictions, a set of encyclopaedias, among other things) were no longer present on the wooden stacks, and instead shoved and stacked haphazardly into various corners of the room. In their old slots were large, old-looking tomes on subjects like zoology, business, ranching, hospitality and a range of other topics equally uncharacteristic of her father. A glance at him, however, revealed that he did not share her surprise at the room's new décor and, on the contrary, seemed quite excited. More importantly, he seemed – at least so she hoped – ready to share with her the purpose for which she had been summoned there.

The pair remained in silence for a short period longer, her confused and him seeming to be on the verge of having his secret burst involuntarily out from him. It was he who first obliged by tossing her a newspaper.

"Take a look at this," said the strong, old man, mastering the excitement that threatened to overtake him.

Virginia took the paper and immediately recognised it as the same she'd read that morning while drinking her coffee.

"What about it?" she answered, in a tone that implied her confusion had not been lessened with the addition of this new piece of information.

"Page six, second article."

Virginia turned to the aforementioned page as instructed and located the article. The title read: *Local Zoo to Be Shuttered!* Again, she remembered this article. Still she was confused.

With the most imploring inflection that she could muster, she replied simply, "So…?"

"So," said the old man, shaking now as his secret poured out of him at last, "I'm going to buy it!" He paused to let her take it in, never taking his eyes off of her, studying her for a hint as to her thought on the matter. When a minute had passed without his daughter uttering a single word, he continued, "Well? What do you think?"

When again she didn't respond, the old man, now wholly overcome with excitement, began gushing without bothering to pause for breath about his plans for the old zoo, the studies he'd undertaken in order to be successful at it, and the joy he would bring to the people and the animals. Virginia sat, dumbstruck and unhearing, as her father's words flowed out of him like an avalanche. She had wondered many things this morning, but the reality of her visit was beyond anything she'd expected, and she was struggling to digest it.

When the old man's words finally began to taper off, it became clear to Virginia that her silence was not something that could be maintained into perpetuity.

She broke it by uttering the following in a choked voice: "What do you mean you're going to buy it?" There was another short pause while she struggled to find her words. "How did you even get this idea? You don't know anything about running a zoo! When did you come up with this? Were you even going to ask me about it?"

The questions fell out on top of each other, and the old man's face dropped a little as he listened. He'd wanted her to be as excited as he was, and here her reaction seemed to suggest that she opposed the idea entirely.

He was, however, sensitive to the shock that he knew his announcement must have produced in his daughter, and so, looking up at her kindly and patiently, he began again: "I may have misspoken, sweetheart. I meant to say that I *bought* the zoo.

7

Already. I'm not *going* to buy it. It's already done." Saying this again gave him the courage to revel in his own excitement, despite her lack of it. "I want you to do this with me, Ginny. Don't you remember how much you used to love the zoo when you were little? How you were always saying that they should do this and that to make the animals happier? Now you can do all those things. You can take care of the animals in a way they've never known before." Here the old man paused momentarily, reading his daughter's expression, but then quickly pressed on. "And, you can take care of the community at the same time by making sure that today's children have the same chance that you did to get to know these creatures. To understand how to respect the right of all things that live on Earth and show compassion to beings that others may view as inferior to themselves. Don't you remember what you learned here and how important it was? Come on, Ginny. Will you do this with me?"

At these pleading words, Ginny's expression softened, and the old man knew that the battle had been won.

While Ginny and her father spoke on about the ludicrous zoo, they were not aware that, across town at the port, a ship bearing the name *Eugenia* and flying an English flag had just entered the harbour. This ship had but one passenger who wore an expression of imperturbable seriousness. He was pale with dark, chin-length hair that was combed back off of his forehead. His eyes were black and intelligent, and his dress was of a time long passed. His vessel crossed the harbour in perfect silence and appeared as though it meant to dock at the public pier when, suddenly, it veered to its starboard side and made its way to a private mooring somewhere off in the distance. Those working at the port took no notice of this abnormal ship, nor its lone captain, as it dropped its anchor into the dark waters of the bay.

-II-

AINSLEY BLAKE STEPPED FROM THE *EUGENIA* ONTO American soil for the first time in his life without so much as a glance around. Being in a new land seemed to have no more effect on him than one might experience upon entering an office of employment, in which they've already spent a long career, on a morning of no marked importance. He seemed wholly unmoved by the prospect of this new adventure. Walking forth from his barge, he began scrutinising his surroundings with no hint of a thrill, but rather with the air of a company owner surveying a plot of land he is thinking of letting in order to expand his operations. To Blake, the New World seemed very much like the Old.

Mr Blake's first order of business, upon his arrival, was a visit to his realtor's office in order to finalise and execute any pending documents regarding his new abode, as well as tie up any loose ends from a legal standpoint. The realtor, although aware of his client's scheduled arrival on that date, had not at all been expecting to see the young man for at least a few days, assuming that after such a long journey (and by sea, no less!), he would be in desperate need of a week's rest at least prior to seeing to any of his unfinished business affairs. This realtor, a pea-shaped, sweaty man called Mr

Davids with a red face, was seated at his immense desk, perusing certain dark corners of the internet, when his intercom sounded, announcing to him how very wrong he had been not to expect his European patron so quickly following his disembarkation.

A bit startled, and hurriedly closing browser windows on his computer screen, he stammered out, "Is that Mr Ainsley Blake, Catherine?"

"Yes, sir, he's only just arrived," replied Catherine, pretending not to notice the hint of alarm in her employer's voice.

"My word! Right then, send him in.

"Mr Blake! Welcome!" said Mr Davids, standing and walking around the side of his desk to greet his visitor.

"Mr Davids, I presume?" replied Blake, taking the chubby hand that was extended to him and shaking it.

"We were so glad to get your referral from our London office, and I hope we have been of some value to you in making your relocation to America as easy and painless as possible," replied Mr Davids, panting a bit with the effort of having risen from his chair and circumnavigated his large wooden desk.

After directing his client to one of the two chairs facing his desk and blotting the sweat from his brow with a large handkerchief, yellowed by frequent use, Mr Davids returned to his own seat and swivelled it around so that the two men were facing each other.

"Drinks!" shouted Mr Davids after a brief moment, as if only just remembering that drinks exist. "I mean, can we get you something to drink?" Without waiting for a reply, he plunged the intercom button with a single pudgy finger, and shouted into the microphone, "Catherine, will you bring us a pitcher of water?" then, turning to Blake, added so that only he could hear, "Perhaps something a bit stronger?" However, seeing that his client didn't take the bait, he returned to the intercom and closed his transmission with a quick, "Thank you, Catherine, just the water for now."

Shortly after, the unerring Catherine arrived with the requested pitcher of water and two clean glasses.

"Now, Mr Blake, there are just a few more signatures that we will need in order to initiate the transfer of any outstanding funds from your overseas account," continued Mr Davids, filling a glass of water and pushing it across the desk to Blake. "Just sign here, here and here. Ah, you'll need a pen, of course! Here it is then. There, that ought to do it!"

Once the vital signatures had been obtained, he stowed them safely away as though he feared his client might demand them back were they left in plain sight for too long, and then paused and eyed Blake attentively. "May I ask what brings you to Georgia, Mr Blake? Forgive me if I'm being too nosey, it's just that we don't get a lot of foreign transplants around here. I'm all for it, of course! The more the merrier and what have you. Just friendly curiosity."

Mr Blake, unmoved, responded without moving his eyes from the blank surface of the desk where the papers had been. "Just looking for a fresh start." After a few more brief moments spent in silence with his head bowed, Blake looked up at Mr Davids again and smiled slightly for the first time, the glass of clear water still sitting untouched in front of him. "It's because there are no other foreigners here that I chose this place."

With that, Blake pushed his borrowed pen back across the desk to the puzzled, bulging realtor and got up from his chair. Mr Davids followed his lead and arose, once again extending his soft hand towards Blake.

"Well we're glad to have you here, sir, whatever the reason, and if you need anything at all, I am wholly at your service."

At this, Blake inclined his head in a slight show of gratitude and exited the office.

-III-

OBADIAH DAVIDS SAT FOR MANY MINUTES IN HIS CHAIR, staring unfixedly in front of him, after his guest had left. He'd never met anyone like that before. Someone so diametrically opposed to himself in character. Blake had been quiet but with none of the apprehension one usually perceives in someone of a traditionally introverted nature. There was no nervousness or intimidation in his eyes, no fear of being so far from his home and alone in a foreign land. The only feeling Mr Davids was confident he had indeed distinguished in his mysterious client's features was one of profound disinterestedness. Who was this fellow that life seemed not to touch?

After another brief moment, Mr Davids rid himself of his discomforting thoughts with a shake of his bulbous head and turned his attention to other matters. Those with an overly gregarious nature tend not to dwell long on those who do not suit their purpose, and a strange and silent newcomer couldn't be expected to take up much of his bother, at least not for any extended period of time. It was especially so tonight, for Mr Davids, with great difficulty and after many previous, failed attempts, had at long last been successful in securing reservations at the new hotspot in town, Chez Sauveur.

Yes, curious fellow indeed. But, what of it? Seems a nice enough sort and let that be the end of it, thought Mr Davids one last time as he grabbed his hat and coat from the rack by his office entryway. Opening the door and stepping into the next room, he turned to bid a good evening to the loyal Catherine, still busy at her desk.

"Any big plans for the evening, my dear?"

"No, sir, just a quiet night with a book," said Catherine.

"Well, what's good for the mind is good for the soul!" said Mr Davids, smiling and jabbing a single fat finger into the air as if propelling his platitude to a level of greater value than it merited. "Good night then, Catherine. Don't forget to lock up and don't stay too late now, hear me?"

"Good night, sir."

Mr Davids exited the building, unaware that he was being watched from across the street. Ainsley Blake eyed the sweaty, waddling man as he made his way from the building, stopping every few paces to catch his breath and mop the sweat from his brow. Blake watched as Mr Davids laboriously climbed into a bright red car that looked almost clownish when juxtaposed with his enormous girth, and exited the small parking lot of the building. Blake thought to himself that Mr Davids might perhaps be someone who would be missed but, on the other hand, was in a state of health that would likely deprive his closest relations of any suspicion that might bring unwanted ire upon himself. The death of a man like Obadiah Davids produces not accusations, but rather justifications in forms like: *Well, he really didn't take very good care of himself,* or: *What can you expect when you let yourself go like that?*

It is, after all, Blake mused, *human nature that we attribute one's death to a problem that is unlikely to threaten ourselves.*

Satisfied with the conclusion already formed in his head, Blake continued on Mr Davids' tail, biding his time with perfect patience as the realtor flew home to prepare for his dinner and vanished inside a small, but ambitiously decorated, house on the town's main street.

When Mr Davids reappeared at his front door, smartly dressed and sweat-free (at least for the time being), the sun had already turned a deep shade of red and begun to drop towards the horizon. Blake waited, expecting the wife he had seen in so many framed pictures back at the realtor's office to appear by his side at any moment, but she never did. Blake had the feeling that Mr Davids hitting the town absent of his wife's company was probably not a rare occurrence and allowed himself a careful exhale of relief. These are the strokes of luck people sometimes refer to as "the little things" which lend to life pleasant moments that serve to break, however fleetingly, the miserable continuity of otherwise dark times. It wasn't that the wife would have presented any real obstacle with regard to Blake's intentions, but Blake was not a bad man and so preferred to avoid any unnecessary bloodshed wherever possible.

The fat realtor closed and locked his front door, crossed his well-manicured front lawn, and climbed, panting, back into his clown car. Blake noticed the beads of sweat reappear on the strained brow and the flabby cheeks that were again reddening with effort. Davids sat for a while, red-faced, fighting to bring his heavy breaths down to a more manageable rhythm before finally cranking the starter and zooming out of his driveway and on to his covert nocturnal rendezvous. Blake proceeded unseen, keeping easy pace with the little car.

After a few blocks, Mr Davids' small, circus-like conveyance disappeared into a vacant parking garage near the centre of town. The garage had been built a few years ago and was still a point of contention among the town's residents. Most had believed it to be an unnecessary use of taxpayer funds, given the small size of the town and its correspondingly modest demand for downtown parking. On the other hand, the town's mayor and downtown business owners had argued that the lack of parking was hurting the town's local economy, and that the additional parking would create the additional demand. With this argument, they had won the day in the end and the garage was approved for immediate construction. Unfortunately for the mayor (and the disastrous re-election campaign that would come later), the time since its completion had, if anything, vindicated the standpoint of its opponents and so it stood, always empty, a relic of a once-vibrant downtown that had never existed in reality.

Blake waited a few minutes after the little car had disappeared into the garage's dark void and then crossed the street and followed it inside. Once he had again located the car within the building, he was forced to immediately throw himself behind one of the numerous concrete support beams in order to remain hidden. To his surprise, the headlights of the car were still shining bright and the front door remained ajar like a single red appendage, akimbo from the car's otherwise uniform body. Something seemed out of place here. Mr Davids, it seemed, was in no rush to exit his vehicle. Wondering why a man who had appeared so eager to be out on the town only moments before was now all of a sudden dawdling, Blake chanced another enquiring look. This time he noticed that he could not see Mr Davids sitting in the car at all, nor standing anywhere around it for that matter. Was it possible that he had already exited the building? And in so much haste that he had neglected to darken his headlights or close his door? It did not seem likely. Blake, exercising caution, slowly moved around the back of the vehicle towards the driver side. The first thing he noticed was a pair of chubby, motionless feet sticking out from the front of the car, one in a loafer of faded and stretched brown leather and the other in a sock of some hideously bright colour pattern, the shoe missing. Had the man succumbed to some cardiovascular attack! Blake had known he was in poor health, but still the odds seemed to favour something more devious. The next thing he saw was a dark figure shoot out from behind the car and towards the street. The figure's speed was so great that it was nothing more than a smudge against a backdrop of setting sun, like a drop of ink on a white sheet of letter paper that has been wiped up hastily and in vain, failing to vanish completely.

Blake watched the figure in total astonishment as it fled away from him and then looked down at the man who lay motionless before him. The vacant eyes of the enormous realtor stared absently away at nothing. The former redness of the pudgy face seemed now to merge with the sweat of his final effort, combining to form the dark liquid now pooling underneath him, reflected invisibly in the red paint of the shiny car. Blake recovered himself.

Before the distance between the mysterious figure and the spectator had grown to a measure that would be beyond recovering, Blake acted. Not daring to hope what this might mean, he pursued the disappearing figure. As he approached and then surpassed the travelling speed of the fleeing figure, and the distance between the two began to close, the dark blur began to come into sharper focus. Blake noticed that the smear he was now gaining on was in fact a man. The man, looking back and realising with absolute stupefaction that he was being pursued by a creature of greater speed than himself, fled helplessly away and in no particular direction. The pair ran through the town's centre, moving so fast that they were virtually unnoticed by the evening revellers who were now beginning to crowd the streets. The only evidence of their presence was a gust of wind and a trail of disturbed earth left in their wake. The two blurred figures would have been perceptible only to those who would have known to look for them, and that was certainly impossible.

After a few minutes of pursuit, Blake overtook the man and, cutting him off, brought him down hard in a tumble of flailing limbs and kinetic energy. When the man opened his eyes and looked up, he saw Ainsley Blake's serious, melancholy figure standing above him, suspicion etched across his stony features in place of the triumph one might expect.

Blake stared down at the panting figure, who was still filthy with the dust of his fall.

"What are you?" Blake asked in a way that implied an answer was compulsory.

The man looked back up at him and suddenly his eyes focused as if he were seeing his pursuer now for the first time.

He stared into Blake's cold eyes and replied simply and with a slight smile, "Well, I am like you, of course. The name's Hugo."

-IV-

"HUGO? WHAT? WHAT DO YOU MEAN YOU'RE LIKE ME? HOW do you move so fast?" Blake demanded, and for the first time in many years, he found that his emotions were not entirely under his control.

The mysterious man once again replied very simply, "I say that Hugo is my name and you know exactly how I can move so fast. Shall I ask you the same silly questions?"

Hugo got up and began dusting himself off. Blake stood, thunderstruck.

"The fat man. Davids. What did you do to him?" asked Blake, reaching for something, anything at all.

Hugo looked up from his dusting. "Ah yes, the chaste Obadiah Davids. I did not do anything to him that his own perverse lifestyle would not have done to him eventually. I am confident that his death will be determined to have occurred from natural causes. I wouldn't worry, my new friend. The death of an Obadiah Davids rarely brings with it enquiries of any depth." Blake contemplated his answer but said nothing, so Hugo continued, "You are stronger than me. Faster. You must be very old." He eyed Blake with a searching gaze.

"I am too old," replied Blake. "I did not think I would ever meet another. At least not now. There are not many left."

Hugo smiled and said, "Well, I guess someone's still making them, for I am not so old as you are." At this he extended a friendly hand to Blake. "Hugo Wegener. Doctor of medical sciences, at least in a former life. And very happy to meet you, my friend."

Blake took the outstretched hand and shook it. "I am called Ainsley Blake."

Once the initial shock had worn off, the two men found themselves, without realising it, retracing their steps back towards the centre of town. This time the two walked side by side, neither in pursuit, neither in flight, at a leisurely pace and began talking of many things. Unsurprisingly, each had many questions for the other.

As the two men walked on, and the impact of the unexpected encounter continued to taper off, Blake began to observe in more detail the strange man now strolling at his left side. Hugo was significantly shorter than he was, and thicker, too. He was not quite fat, but someone about whom one might say: *He could stand to lose a few.* He had lighter hair than Blake, a kind of sandy blond mess but darker, almost brown. He was good-natured and Blake could tell that in his former life, perhaps many years ago, he probably would have been the funny one among his group of friends. He had a particular way of speaking that was enjoyable for the listener. It seemed like every sentence was punctuated at the end with "my friend", and his speech had a jovial frankness that Blake found irresistibly refreshing. *Jolly.* That was the word for it. He was jolly. Short, pot-bellied and laughing. Or at least he was the ghost of jolly from a past life. No one in his position could be jolly still. Not after what he'd probably had to do to stay alive. But one could see that he had been jolly, sometime in the past, and the impact of that period of his life was still tangible in his present character.

As the pair continued walking, they passed many of the town's residents out enjoying their evenings in the pleasant night air. The foot traffic seemed to have increased in kind with the darkening sky, but no one seemed to pay the slightest bit of attention to the two men walking together, though both were strangers. It was not unusual, after all, for people from the neighbouring rural areas to come into town for an evening of revelry and, since the two men were obviously not from the town, it was only natural that the assumption made regarding their presence would be that which was the most obvious. The two men walked on, aware of and enjoying their privacy, talking liberally and growing more comfortable. Blake could not remember a time when he had ever spoken so much and on such topics. Considering this further, however, he checked himself and sought to reign in the liberality that was threatening to tear down the personal defences he had spent years constructing. Vulnerability was something that Ainsley Blake had learned long ago to avoid, and now he found himself slipping in the face of a near-stranger. Hugo, perceiving none of the internal struggle playing out next to him, spoke on in excited outpourings of language. It was clear that he too had gone a length of time without a proper conversation and he pushed on as though this might be his only chance and he was determined not to waste it.

They continued walking and talking on absentmindedly until Hugo suddenly felt his forward progress halted by a single, black-sleeved arm. He looked up to the arm's owner and saw Blake no longer at ease, staring off into the distance at something, not moving a muscle.

-V-

GINNY HARRISON AND HER LOVING FATHER WALKED ARM in arm towards the movie theatre at the centre of town just as the sun was beginning to set. The earlier argument about the zoo had been won by the old man, as she had known all along it would be, and the two had not mentioned it since. It was their custom to avoid revisiting the outcomes of their arguments in the immediate aftermath of their resolutions and, accordingly, their day had been spent in a very normal fashion following the surprising revelations of that morning. She and her father had decided to make a go of the zoo and, when the conviction in the old man's voice had at last convinced her that the argument was beyond saving, the topic of conversation had shifted automatically and effortlessly to that of where they should eat lunch, since it had been about that time anyway. After lunch, the two of them spent the rest of the afternoon tidying up the old man's study, because Ginny had said that it looked like it had been ransacked. The exaggerated comment had made the old man smile and so he consented with mock distress to an afternoon of cleaning with the daughter that so delighted his heart. Now, with the evening approaching, the two made their way towards the movie theatre for yet another of their favourite family activities.

The old man ambled down the sidewalk, guiding his daughter, full of gratitude and happiness for her whom he so loved and the new enterprise that he was about to set out upon with her by his side. Things had aligned themselves within his life in such a way that he had considered that he had no right to expect so much good fortune and was therefore determined to be worthy of it. They walked and laughed and she leaned on his shoulder. They talked about the movies that were out and which one they might see. He pretended to resist when she'd nominated some sort of teen love comedy as a potential film candidate for the night, knowing all too well that he would happily see whatever movie she wanted with pleasure.

As they neared the theatre, Ginny felt her father slow his pace at her side and begin to fall behind. Within a few seconds he had stopped walking completely. She looked over at him and saw that he was standing still, his gaze frozen on some point in the distance. She looked in the same direction but didn't see anything other than what looked like a recently trodden trail in the pristine grass of the vast quad. A narrow parting of the otherwise undisturbed and uniform evening dew. Probably just some stray animal's ritual commute across the town's main square on its way back to the woods after a long day of pillaging dumpsters. Certainly nothing out of the ordinary.

"Are you alright, Dad?" asked Ginny, confused.

The old man seemed to snap back to himself. "Yes, sweetheart. Sorry about that. I thought I saw something."

He rejoined her and fell quickly back into stride alongside her. They continued on amicably and, soon after, arrived at the theatre. All smiles again, and having now settled officially on the teen love comedy as the final movie decision, despite the old man's affected protestations, Ginny went to the ticket window to purchase their seats. The transaction was concluded quickly and she turned back to her father, surprised to find him once again in the same trance, staring straight ahead into the distance. Again, she followed his gaze with her own eyes. This time she did not simply see empty space but instead two strangely dressed men standing side by side. One was taller and lean, the other shorter and heavy-set. Of these two men, only one was staring back in their direction, and he did so with an almost identical expression to that of her father – one of surprise, fear and mistrust. The shorter man had seemed not to notice that his friend had stopped walking at first but soon realised and looked up himself.

Ginny tapped her father's shoulder softly. "Do you know those guys, Dad?"

The old man, again seeming to snap back from somewhere distant and return to himself, said to the worried girl, "No, Ginny, I don't know them. I'm sure they're just in town for the evening. I shouldn't have been staring. Nothing to worry about at all, sweetheart."

Ainsley Blake met the staring eyes, wondering why an old man whom he had never met before was glaring at him so intently. It was impossible that this man knew anything about him or had been able to perceive the chase that had ensued between him and Hugo only minutes before. Blake was a complete stranger to this man, and he knew it. After a few uncomfortable moments spent returning the old man's glare, Blake consoled himself by remembering that older people seemed to have a universal tendency to violate the rules of politeness when it came to observing things foreign or out of place, especially when those things interrupt the routine of their normal lives. In this small, Georgian town, Ainsley Blake was certainly out of place, and so he dismissed his suspicions of the bizarre exchange and thought no more of it. Instead, he turned his attention to the young woman standing at the old man's side. Instantly he was blown away, caught off guard by her beauty. Her brunette hair, the grace and fluidity of her movements, and her eyes, though full of concern for the old man, still smiling and golden – he had never seen her equal. Or perhaps he had, once, a

23

long time ago. The ancient heart, long atrophied in his chest, gave a triumphant lurch, rebelling against the silence that had been so long imposed upon it. It seemed to be grasping for life anew, a strange sensation. Unfamiliar. Blake had almost forgotten what it was like. What *it* was exactly, he wasn't sure. The only thing he knew for certain was that *it* was dangerous. He had lived long enough to know that.

-PART TWO-

- I -

G INNY HARRISON SAT AT HER KITCHEN TABLE READING
  her paper and drinking her coffee. Periodically, she paused
in her reading to reflect on the events of the previous day and, each
time she did so, she found herself assigning greater significance
to them. First, there had been her father's casual declaration that
he would be purchasing, refurbishing and then reopening a zoo.
Then, as if that wasn't enough to meet the day's quota of strange,
there was his bizarre reaction to the two strangers they had seen at
the movies.

Of course, with regard to the zoo, no further discussion beyond
the initial declaration of its purchase had occurred in regards to
practical things like who would manage it, or how, but her father
had seemed so unconcerned about the logistics of it at the time
that she had contented herself merely wallowing silently in shock
as opposed to unleashing the innumerable protestations that her
reason would have otherwise demanded. However, now that a full
night had passed and she was alone, she was able to reflect on
the situation of the zoo more reasonably and – more importantly
– away from her father and the unconquerable expression he
had worn on his face while he was telling her, both excited and

pleading. Reflecting on the prospect of a zoo now, in her kitchen with her coffee, the absurdity of the whole project washed over her anew. It had been ridiculous from the outset and the only thing that remained was to find a way to tell him without breaking his heart. Secretly, she hoped that time might erode his will, and perhaps even do the job for her. She would gently push him in the direction of more readily attainable pursuits once the project of the zoo revealed itself to be more of a challenge than perhaps he had initially imagined. For now, however, she reasoned that she would just go along with it and she would soon find out what the future held.

As for the two unknowns that they had encountered in town, she could not make heads or tails of it. With the zoo, she was able to at least partially attribute it to an old man's boredom, or perhaps a last-ditch effort at achieving something novel in a life grown sedentary with age. Maybe even a late-occurring mid-life crisis, or some act of rebellion against the inevitable march of time. The psychology of that was feasible to her, but the look on her father's face when he'd seen those two men in town was something she had never seen there before. There had been fear in it, and she had never seen him afraid. Even as an old man there was nothing that frightened him. He was the strongest man she knew, even now, and had always been so.

She meditated on these things until her attention span was exhausted and then put them aside for deliberation at a later time. For now, she made peace with it by reminding herself that the strange occurrences of the previous day were perhaps only so because of their close proximity to one another and, had they occurred on separate months or even days, they would have been far less startling than they were having occurred almost simultaneously. This thought comforted her a great deal and it wasn't long before her morning routine began to assume the form of those that had generally preceded it each day over the last five years. She read her *paper* paper, drank her coffee, and soon the glowing smile that defined her appeared again on her lovely face.

At 9:30 sharp she closed the front door behind her and set out. She smiled dutifully at the neighbour, who smiled back.

"Good morning, Ginny!"

She answered with another smile and it was more than enough. Today there was no unexpected meeting with her father and, though she relished the moments spent with him, this gave her peace. Today was hers and she revelled in it, though not too much. The guilt that her current good mood was attained by means of temporarily disregarding her father's dream was ever-present in the back of her mind and, being Ginny Harrison, that was no small thing.

- II -

P ROUST WAS ONE OF ONLY A HANDFUL OF COFFEE SHOPS IN
the entire town, and Ginny Harrison's personal favourite. It
was named Proust for two reasons. The first was that the town
fancied itself French in a lot of cultural aspects, though the bulk
of its inhabitants were of German descent. And, while it was true
that the townspeople never outright claimed to be French, they
did not often boast publicly of their German heritage either. As a
result, French culture was allowed to be largely appropriated, and
places like Proust and Chez Sauveur were born. Despite its name,
Proust was the only coffee shop remaining not yet ruined by the
influence of an ever-growing population of hipsters. Ginny liked
it because when she ordered a large, black coffee, that is exactly
what she got. There were none of the frills or complications that
plagued the other shops in town where, in order to get a simple
coffee, one needed first to be fluent in an entirely new language
created for the sole purpose of communicating with modern-
day baristas. At Proust, there was no such thing as a grande iced
caramel macchiato, double whipped with agave nectar, and to ask
for such a thing would only serve to confuse the waitress. Proust
also had other attributes beyond its refreshing simplicity that

attracted Ginny. For one, and this was the second reason for its being named Proust, the walls were lined with books that were free for perusal by the shop's patrons, classical fiction mostly, and the seating provided was soft, comfortable and plentiful. For obvious reasons, this place was a lot more Ginny's speed than some place desperately striving for hipness and only ruining itself in the process.

Today she sat perched in her usual seat, absentmindedly combing through a mass market paperback edition of *Silas Marner* by her all-time favourite author, George Eliot, whom she always referred to by her given name, Mary Anne Evans. She had a fondness for fiction and especially those women in history who had penned some of its best: the Brontë sisters, Jane Austen, Virginia Woolf and, of course, the aforementioned Mary Anne Evans, among others. She admired them as much for their accomplishments against great odds as for the extraordinary quality of their words. They had succeeded supremely in a field and time dominated by men. Mary Evans had felt so oppressed by her sex, in fact, that she had assumed the pen name (or *nom de plume*, as it might have been called at any of the other coffee shops in town) George Eliot, simply so that her work would be given due consideration. And what a loss it would be for the world had it not been. Ginny loved this about these women and aspired in her own life to emulate their strength in everything she did. When she felt like giving up, or was even just in need of a reminder as to why she was who she was, she drew fresh inspiration from their words and, in that pursuit, spent many mornings lost amongst their pages at Proust.

After an hour or so of deep meditation in the company of her favourite authors, Ginny, with effort, forced herself up and on to the events of the day. She paid her bill, tipping amply as always, and bid the wait staff goodbye. When she stepped outside, the heat of the day had already swelled and was drawing a steady breeze from the sea that wound all throughout the small town. She thought to herself how stifling the town would be were it not for that steadfast breeze that was ever-present and so familiar to her. She was grateful for it, as she was grateful for everything, as happy young women often are when their lives have given them no cause for pain and every reason for gratitude.

Ginny walked quickly down the sidewalk, but not as someone in a hurry might. Her strides were full of purpose and their speed was to some noble end rather than an indication of tardiness. She was headed to work now and she knew that today she had a lot of it. Ginny worked a light schedule – on weekdays only – doing administrative work for one of the private marinas in town owned by a Mr GW Dobbs. The "GW" stood for George Washington, but Dobbs disliked that fact so much that he insisted everyone call him "Dub". Dub was exactly what one might expect in someone who owned a marina – tank-topped, unshaven and portly. He wore a jumpsuit perpetually (the same one, if you were to ask anyone in town) and the top half of it always hung loose around his waist as if he had removed a dirty, threadbare sweater and tied it there for safekeeping. He smoked Marlboro Reds constantly, walked with a slight limp and cursed (although he was always quick to apologise for it in front of Ginny). Most of all, however, he was kind. Salty, but immensely kind, and he loved Ginny like she was his own daughter.

Ginny had been working at the marina for four years, ever since Dub had lost his wife to cancer. Mrs Dobbs had been an enormously large woman with a comparably large heart and it was she who had always been the business side of Dub's marina operation. He'd always said that she was better at talking to people, and he was better at filling gas tanks and shaving barnacles off of boat propellers. When she had gotten sick, Ginny had volunteered to help out around the marina and, after her death, it had become a permanent thing.

Ginny arrived at the marina around 11am, still holding her to-go cup from Proust, and found Dub already immersed in the day's work and perceptibly irritable. It was going to be an especially busy day because the marina had taken in a new vessel the day before, which always meant a lot of paperwork. First and foremost, the ship logs had to be brought up to date. Then, at least with the larger boats, there was usually cargo that would have to remain on board for a period of time, under the care of the marina, until it could finally be offloaded by the owners and transferred to its final destination. This meant agreements had to be signed, insurance carriers notified, inventories taken and security measures considered. The whole process ran through Ginny's head as she sat down in her small, waterfront office to get started while Dub galumphed frantically around the docks tending to their other clients' property still in need of service.

Ginny grabbed the new arrival's manifest from the inbox on her desk and began reading.

Vessel Name: *Eugenia*
Point of Embarkation: *London, England*
Point of Arrival: *Georgia, United States*
Passengers: *0*
Crew: *1 (Captain)*
Cargo…

Etc., etc., and so on and so forth.

She scrolled down the list, noticing that the contents of the ship's hull seemed to be of a personal rather than commercial nature, but this was certainly not out of the ordinary for a sailing vessel like the *Eugenia*. Commercial ships were generally powered by means of a mechanical engine, they being far more reliable than fickle ocean winds. After all, their owners are not generally given to entrusting their fates (nor their profits) to the whims of gods.

It was only after fully updating the marina logs and inputting the ship's entire manifest that Ginny realised how quiet it had become since she had started working. Dub's usually frequent interruptions were conspicuously absent and, accustomed to working in noise, Ginny often found silence unnerving, or worse, an indication of trouble. Rising from her desk and looking around, it didn't take long before she spotted Dub out on the pier, seemingly engaged in animated conversation with someone positioned just out of sight. She turned back to her computer, saved her work and then exited the small office out onto the pier.

As Ginny skipped down the rickety pier towards her employer, careful to avoid any of the splintered planks or exposed nails that she knew by heart to be present along her path, she noticed that the sailboat he now stood in front of was none other than that which had arrived in harbour the previous day. She saw the vessel's great masts and the name, *Eugenia*, etched in gold lettering on its side just under the bow. It really was a magnificent ship (even more so because she knew it was likely a private vessel) black, sleek and stately. It bore none of the scars one might expect to find on a ship of that size that had just completed a transatlantic journey. It almost looked freshly scrubbed. It occurred to her that its lone captain must have been very fortunate with regard to weather for, even these days, a solo trip across the Atlantic in a sailboat is no small feat.

When she arrived at Dub's side and swung her gaze portside to the far end of the ship, she at last saw the man with whom he had been so excitedly engaged. She recognised him instantly and would have fallen over into the harbour with surprise had Dub's sturdy arm not come to her rescue. The lone captain was none other than the mysterious stranger who had so alarmed her father the night before. His smaller, squatter sidekick did not appear to be present, but here *he* was, just as he had been before, but different too in a way. *He* who had returned her father's gaze and shared his same expression of fear, surprise and mistrust. It had been *he* who had entered the town's harbour the previous day, alone on a sailing vessel from England, and now he stood before her. His expression was not remotely similar to that which had tormented her since the night before. Instead, he seemed to be enjoying himself, talking with Dub. He was quiet and smiling, listening politely to Dub drone on about the fish in England versus Georgia. And then on to the fish on the Eastern Coast of the US as opposed to those on the Pacific side (the West Coast folks didn't know how to fish properly, in Dub's opinion, and were doing more harm than good). The stranger seemed genuinely entertained by Dub's rough edges, simplicity, stubborn opinions, and lack of verbal filter. Once Ginny had approached, however, she could sense that his point of focus had shifted, though his eyes never left Dub's face while he spoke.

After Ginny's fall, and Dub's subsequent show of heroism in rescuing her, the two men paused their conversation to acknowledge the newcomer, as was dictated by their good manners.

"What happened there, Gin?" Dub asked as he pulled her upright again, making sure that she had her footing before releasing her. "C'mon, I got ya."

Ginny stabilised herself, now more embarrassed than surprised, and said, "Just lost my footing, Dub. Thanks for not letting me go into the water."

"You need to be more careful!" replied Dub sternly before changing the subject and indicating the stranger next to him. "This fella is an Englishman and he sailed this ship all the way from London. Says he's not a fisherman, though, but I guess we forgive him that sin!" At this, Dub let out a booming laugh that quickly dissolved into a fit of coughs.

He waved Ginny off when she stooped to help him. "I'm fine. I said I'm fine, dammit!"

Ginny backed off and allowed Dub to rein in his coughing fit without the benefit of her assistance. Instead, she turned to the stranger.

He looked back at her, smiling softly with an amused look, and said, "I am Ainsley Blake."

-III-

GINNY HARRISON LOOKED BACK INTO THE EYES OF AINSLEY Blake, completely unaware of how confused and silly she looked.

This was not lost on Blake, who promptly said in reply to her expression, "I'm so sorry, but have we met somewhere before?"

He knew very well that they had not formally met, but that he had seen her the night before, and that she was that unique creature whom had so unexpectedly stirred his long-forgotten heart. He pressed her with his glare until she seemed to snap out of her confusion.

She smiled politely at him and said, "No, I don't think so. I've never been to England before." As an afterthought she added to herself, "Or anywhere really, for that matter." Blake persisted silently in his soft, unbroken gaze until she went on. "Have you ever been to the United States before?"

"I never have," replied Blake. "Yesterday marked the first time I have ever set foot on American soil."

Ginny studied him, still with her polite smile. "Well, we're happy to have you here. It's very nice to meet you!" Her hand shot out stiffly and he took it, shook it and dropped it.

Ginny continued, "Do you mind following me, please? I have some papers for you to sign. Can I assume you will be leaving the ship here for the time being with its cargo intact?"

Blake gave her a slight nod, which told her that she could indeed assume, and extended one of his arms out before them, palm upturned, indicating that she need only lead the way and he would follow her. Recognising this universal gesture, she performed a swift about-face and set off again towards her office, now with Ainsley Blake in tow, leaving Dub looking slightly bewildered, but on the whole unconcerned, on the docks behind them.

The paperwork didn't take long once they got to the office. Mr Blake seemed familiar with legalities of the type and Ginny was certainly efficient with regard to the whole process, having mastered it over the past four years. As they went through everything, and she spoke more to the newcomer, she slowly began to let her guard drop. He didn't seem like a bad man, nor one that she needed to be suspicious of, and she was soon able to attribute the strangeness of the previous evening to nothing more than an over-thinking on her part of something that had been nothing in reality. She studied him as he read and signed various documents and noticed that a change had come over him since they had been outside. The look of quiet amusement that he had worn throughout his intercourse with Dub had shifted now to one of melancholy and evasiveness. He asked questions but avoided her eyes when he did so. It seemed that as her guard dropped, his rose. Determined not to again fall victim to the over-analysation of a non-issue, she brushed it off and resolved to remain professional and finish the job rather than torture herself dwelling on the irrelevant mood swings of a stranger. With the papers signed, and terms agreed upon, the business was concluded, and the two of them rose and exited the small office back into the warm sea breeze.

Once back on the pier Blake turned to Ginny and thanked her.

He shook her hand again and met her eyes for the first time since they had left Dub, then asked, "I'd like to thank Mr Dobbs as well. Do you know where he might have gone?"

"Oh, sure, he's out here somewhere," Ginny answered. "Probably just messing with one of the other boats. The work never really stops around here. C'mon, I'll help you find him."

As they walked along the row of boats together in search of Dub, Ginny stood on her tiptoes, arching her neck in a futile attempt to gain the height necessary to see over the docked vessels. Despite her best efforts, however, they continued to tower stubbornly over her, obstructing her view. After a few minutes of fruitless searching, Ginny's brow began to furl and, unable to spot Dub amongst the various moored ships, she decided to stop and listen instead. After all, Dub could usually be heard grumbling or cursing under his breath when all else was quiet. To her dismay, after a minute of silence she still could not locate him. All was still.

As Blake continued his search throughout the multitude of boats, not entirely sure which of them had already been checked, Ginny veered off the main pier to search an adjacent dock that was rarely used. What Blake heard next was a blood-curdling scream, cleaving the stillness like an atom bomb, and within seconds his protective instincts had involuntarily carried him to its source at Ginny's side. He looked first at her horrified face and then followed her gaze down to a silent, seizing figure on the ground. It was Dub, twisted and convulsing, having an apparent seizure and sprawled out on the dock. Though he had not fallen into the water, his purpling face and terrible silence immediately told Blake that he could not breathe.

Ginny looked on in horror as the beloved old man inched towards death at her feet. Blake, with an unnatural calm, bent down at the old man's side and studied him seriously but did nothing at first. Right when Ginny thought the old man had reached his end and was entering death's final throes, Blake plunged a pale hand into the gaping mouth and then abruptly pulled it out again, wiping thick saliva off on the front of his double-breasted coat. Ginny, for reasons she could not understand, chose this moment to notice for the first time how unfitting his attire was for the warm weather and, still wondering how she'd missed noticing it before, thought how odd and inappropriate it was that she should take note of something so trivial during something so serious. To her immense relief, however, the withdrawal of Blake's hand seemed to once again permit air to re-enter Dub's gasping lungs. Blake allowed the old man to take several life-saving gulps of air before promptly turning him on his side so that he might ride out the remainder of his episode in relative safety. The two young people stood side by side, speechless, and watched the old man intently for signs of improvement. Ginny didn't realise that she had involuntarily put her hand on Blake's forearm to steady herself, though Blake had noticed immediately. He would have moved his arm and stepped away, had sympathy for the traumatised girl not held him fast where he stood. After two or three more minutes, Dub's gasping breaths began to level out and become less erratic. The convulsions too seemed to taper off and finally Dub lay still, drawing steady, unlaboured breaths on the dock, the normal colouration of his face slowly returning. The immediate danger, it appeared, was averted.

After another couple of minutes, the old marina owner's eyelids began to flutter and he regained consciousness.

He looked up at the two faces staring down at him and said weakly, "What happened?"

Ginny opened her mouth to speak but found that she had no voice. Instead she burst into tears and dropped down to her knees, trapping Dub in a hug so tight that it threatened to suffocate him all over again.

Blake too kneeled beside them and began to explain. "Have you ever had a seizure before?"

"Never!" insisted Dub, somewhat indignant. "And I'm not planning to start now!"

Blake examined the bump on his head and continued, "What's the last thing you remember?"

"Well, I came over to this dock to get some tools I'd left here this morning and the next thing I know, here I am."

Dub looked around confusedly as he explained, desperately trying to pull answers regarding his precarious situation from the air. Blake got up and began examining the wooden beams of the dock. A few feet away from where Dub had fallen he found the offending piece of wood for which he had been searching. Rotted, loose and very recently splintered.

Turning back to Dub, he offered his theory: "It looks to me like you tripped on this rotted beam here and had a bad fall." Blake indicated the split piece of wood to the two listeners and then elaborated. "When you fell, I'm guessing you hit your head pretty hard, at least judging by that knot coming out over your left temple, and I suspect that's probably what caused your seizure. Mr Dobbs, you need to get to a doctor right away. If you have a concussion, you will need medical attention immediately, and you don't want to have another seizure while no one is here to help you. You could have just as easily ended up in the water and, had that been the case, it would have been unlikely that we would have been able to find you in time."

Ainsley Blake and Virginia Harrison, forever connected now by the bonds of a great trial overcome together, helped the weak old man to his feet. To their mutual delight, it appeared that Dub had regained his former irritability and, cursing under his breath, was complaining more about what would become of his marina while he was gone, rather than his close brush with death. Ginny reassured him that she would look after everything, while Blake shouldered the bulk of the old man's heft. They walked him to Ginny's car and, after putting him in the backseat, Ginny turned to Blake with tears in her eyes. Despite her tears, however, her voice was steady.

"I don't know how to thank you for what you did today." She paused, fighting back against the emotion that was welling up from her heart. "I don't know what would have happened if you hadn't been here."

Blake looked at her kindly and said, "Don't worry, I think he will be just fine now. He seems to have a very strong will to live and that goes a long way. Longer than most people would give it credit for."

Ginny smiled sadly at him and said, "Well, I'm going to take him to the doctor's office now. Thanks again." She turned to leave but stopped and looked back at him one more time. "You know, if you want someone to show you around town sometime, I'd be happy to. You've only just come here and it is the least I can do."

Blake looked nervous but managed to say, "Yes, we will see," before turning and heading briskly off in the opposite direction like a spooked bovine.

- IV -

I N THE WEEKS THAT FOLLOWED THE MARINA OWNER'S BRUSH
with death, the small, Georgian town was absolutely teeming
with gossip. After all, in a town where everyone knows everyone
else, good pieces of gossip are a valuable social currency. In the
immediate aftermath of Dub's episode, the streets were filled with
whispers regarding the events that had transpired and, most of all,
regarding the role and identity of the unknown stranger who had
miraculously saved the day. The description of the story varied
based on who was telling it, but they all included some version
of the truth, no matter how convoluted it got. The most absurd
adaption, by far, had been that the stranger had somehow managed
to attack Dub in order to free himself from the obligation of
paying his bill. On the other end of the spectrum was a variation
of the story that was probably – at least of the many in circulation
– the closest to the actual truth, since a truly accurate account
of what had transpired seemed to have eluded the whole of the
speculating townspeople entirely. According to this version, the
stranger had, quite fortuitously, just happened to be a doctor, and
was therefore able to apply his medical skill to the afflicted Dub
just in the nick of time. With these two stories and every iteration

that fell in between them, it seemed that the town would not be letting go of the affair anytime soon and whichever version of the story it was, Ainsley Blake wanted none of it.

Instead, he spent the weeks of his minor celebrity status locked away in his house, not daring to venture out. Fortunately, the only members of his new community that possessed any knowledge of his potential whereabouts were those with whom he had conducted some sort of business, and so were forbidden by the confidential nature of their formal relationship to divulge his address to anyone who might be seeking it.

Though his solitude was not likely to be threatened by uninvited guests and, moreover, he believed that all the hysteria would soon pass with little in the way of any permanent effect, he could not help but curse himself for his own carelessness in having come to the aid of the old man. He had relocated to the New World to start fresh and the last thing he needed was to draw attention to himself. He had simply reacted in the heat of the moment and intervened in the old man's fate without thinking. He knew he had done so because of the girl and began to think again how dangerous she truly was to him. Because of her, an entire town was now talking about him, seeking him out, and all this madness had begun when he had barely been off his ship for twenty-four hours. Now, weeks later, he paced his house in agony and waited for time to once again obscure him from the world.

During this period in which Blake remained exiled almost entirely from the outside community at large, there was one person with whom he did keep up a regular correspondence. The good doctor, Hugo Wegener, was a frequent visitor to the sprawling manor house, and had been ever since their chance meeting on Blake's first evening in town. He brought with him his jovial manner, the only solace that Blake could rely upon in his solitude, and quickly showed himself to be an invaluable friend. The two men, both wise from an overabundance of experience, engaged each other on an almost equal footing, and their conversations often lasted for hours on end. It seemed that neither of them had held a conversation of any value in a very long time and, finding themselves finally challenged and able to flex the muscles of their intellect, simply could not stop once started. Such was the delight of the two men that Hugo's visits became a near-daily occurrence.

One day, a few weeks after their initial meeting, Hugo was sitting at Blake's stately dining table, perusing an ancient volume of Eastern European folklore, when Blake entered the room and joined him. Whenever he was at Blake's residence, Hugo could, more often than not, be found in the same spot, lost inside some great book, just so long as he was not otherwise occupied elsewhere. One of the things Hugo loved most about his visits to Blake's manor was the access it gave him to its vast library. Contained within it were all manner of printed works, some of which Hugo knew to be extremely valuable. Blake had first edition copies of some of literature's most famous works (some even contained hand-written dedications by their authors), ancient texts that had been inked by steady hands in beautiful calligraphy and unpublished manuscripts that were purported to be authored by literary giants. The collection was so vast and so impressive that Hugo dedicated a portion of each visit to its perusal. It was not uncommon that Blake would venture in during these sessions to join him, and Hugo always welcomed the intrusion as Blake could always be counted upon to answer questions regarding the books' origins that their pages could not. On this particular occasion, however, Blake brought with him a copy of the local newspaper and thrust it inconsiderately in between the doctor's face and the volume of European folklore he had been reading.

"Have you seen?" Blake asked. "It says the fat man died of a heart attack."

Hugo looked down at the paper and then up at Blake. "Of course it does, my friend. It is because a heart attack is what killed our dear Mr Davids."

Blake eyed him suspiciously and asked, "What do you mean he died of a heart attack? I was there."

"I mean that he died of a heart attack," said Hugo placidly. Seeing that Blake looked as confused as ever and now angry, Hugo explained, "Obadiah Davids was not a healthy man, my dear friend. He was grossly overweight. He drank profusely, ate poorly and smoked cigars. Through all of this he suffered heart palpitations and chest pain but neglected his symptoms. The rest is there in the paper. He suffered a fatal heart attack. If I had to guess, I'd say that it was likely brought on by a sudden, unexpected drop in blood pressure, accompanied, of course, by over-stress." Hugo glanced quickly back down at the article and then looked up again at Blake. "And it appears that his external wounds are being attributed to the subsequent fall that inevitably followed in the wake of his fatal coronary episode." Hugo watched Blake and smiled as he saw the comprehension dawn on his friend's face. "I told you, my friend. Hugo Wegener, doctor of medical sciences, at your service."

-V-

THE WEEKS THAT FOLLOWED WERE SOME OF THE MOST
enjoyable that Blake could remember having in his own
recent history, even when viewed in conjunction with his current
self-imposed imprisonment. He had avoided people for so long
that he had forgotten how truly important their company was
to a person's well-being. He wondered, too, whether or not it
would have been possible to have found a friendship so mutually
enjoyable, were the man on the other side of it not stricken with
the same uncommon affliction as himself. Was it only because
they were both cursed by a mutual source of unending life that
they needed each other, or was their connection less superficial?
Perhaps their relationship was so unique and valuable because
they each possessed the cumulative, though differing, wisdom
of lifetimes, and could therefore converse on an equal footing.
A kind of conduit through which each man could learn and
be challenged after so many tedious years spent wallowing in
intellectual stagnation. Blake thought about these things often
but, in the end, decided that they were of no consequence, as
the friendship was invaluable to his own sanity, at the very least
while he rode out the storm that had been spawned in the wake

of Dub's rescue. Eventually, he even went so far as to declare to himself that it would actually be better for all involved parties were their friendship to be based on selfish, individual pleasures, fleeting as they were, rather than any genuine feeling of regard that might risk permanency. After all, in Blake's experience, it was always best to keep people at an arm's length.

Hugo Wegener, for his part, never thought about their friendship in terms of the potential danger it posed to himself. He never thought in such terms because, though he had lived many years, he had never been in a dangerous position of adequate severity, nor with enough frequency, to necessitate such considerations of self-preservation above all else. Hugo had not yet been made to learn the lessons that so many who had come before him, and indeed his new friend, Blake, had been forced to. On the contrary, his days with Blake were spent largely in gratitude for his newfound companion. He strolled the grounds of the manor house smiling pleasantly, in a state of worriless contentment that was far purer and simpler than one might think possible in a man possessed of his considerable intellectual gifts.

One day, two months after Blake had first instituted his self-imposed incarceration, the two men found themselves at their usual table, casually studying one of the great volumes of Blake's library. The mood had been exceptionally jovial that morning due to a piece of favourable news the pair had received in the day's local paper. According to the article, it appeared that Mr George Washington Dobbs had made a full recovery at a hospital in Atlanta and had returned to town in full health to reassume the management of his beloved marina which had, during his convalescence, been looked after by his long-time and beloved employee, Ms Virginia Harrison. What this news meant for Blake was a conclusion to the story that had so plagued him. The return of Dub meant a concrete end to the saga of his collapse and subsequent rescue by a mysterious stranger that had so enraptured the town. With Dub's recovery would follow inevitably the town's apathy, because a healthy Dub was not in need of rescue, and people would therefore forget quickly that one had ever taken place. This news meant imminent freedom for Ainsley Blake.

A few days prior to the date he had settled upon for his liberation found Blake again reading through the local newspaper. He had read it every week since his arrival in town and had been able to gain by it knowledge of just about every one of his new neighbours. Being a small town with little in the way of what larger cities might consider to be "real" news, the small local paper filled most of its pages with stories on its own modest reader base, including editorials written by the same. There were stories on things like Ms Dolores Fischer's cats (which the article sympathetically stated were her only remaining source of companionship, since her adored and only son had broken her heart by leaving town in order to participate in a study abroad programme), Mr Frederick Muller's generous contributions to the town's maritime society, Mr Thomas Becker's record-breaking shrimp yield or Mr Jonathan Lange's failing health. It was the last of these stories that piqued Blake's interest now in the twilight of his concealment. The article had painted a picture of Jonathan Lange as a solitary man, without friends or family (save a long-deceased wife), who had grown so mean in his elderly years that no one ever visited him, even now in the throes of his final illness. When he had been discovered unconscious on his living-room floor, it was only because an employee of the power company, who had been sent to cut the power when it became clear that the old hermit had no intention of paying his bills, had chanced upon a window that looked in on the room where the man had fallen. By means of a slightly ajar curtain, the shocked employee was able to perceive the prone figure motionless on the floor and proceeded to alert the proper authorities. The article went on to explain that Mr Lange was a man of considerable wealth, and since he and his wife had had no children, nor had any other heir ever been designated, a debate had broken out amongst the townspeople regarding what might become of the sizeable estate. Most speculated that, given the estate's enormous value, some long-lost relative would materialise at the moment of death and lay claim to the old man and their inheritance. Others remembered, or at least thought they did, times during which they had shown kindness to the old man back when he had still been healthy. These people chose to hope that, based on the compassion they had shown in comparison to the cruelty of all the rest, the old man would remember them, and perhaps they would be rewarded. Of course, the reality of the matter was that these people had shown no more kindness to the old man than had anyone else but, unlike everybody else, they were possessed with misplaced optimism – that same mental defect found in those who play the lottery every cycle or chronic gamblers.

Blake folded the newspaper and sat back in contemplation of what he had read when a knock sounded at his front door. His first thought was that it must be Hugo, but he quickly dismissed that notion knowing that Hugo no longer knocked, being now so familiar to the house. Confused and unable to think of a single person who might have a need to visit him, he made his way slowly to the front atrium and, swinging the heavy door on its hinges, met his surprise visitor with shock.

Reluctantly, Ainsley Blake looked up into the shining eyes of a nervously smiling Ginny Harrison. Still recovering from the great internal jolt that he had suffered upon seeing her and struggling with all his power to repress any outward sign of it, Blake did not return her smile immediately. In his heart, he knew that there was no one whom he would have rather found on the other side of his own door, but outwardly he fought desperately to appear unmoved. She looked as lovely as she had at the movie theatre, at the docks, and even in his own mind's eye where one's memory of something cherished is often exaggerated in comparison to its existence in reality. On the contrary, Blake found that she looked even more beautiful now than ever had that internal version of her that he carried within himself and allowed to reign supreme over his every thought. Even when Dub had been suffering, Blake had found that the purity of Ginny's concern for her friend had moved him. Looking at her now, Blake realised with urgency, and a little embarrassment, that at least a full minute had already elapsed since her arrival on his doorstep, and he had still not yet managed to utter a single word.

Virginia Harrison, feeling slightly less courageous in the wake of Blake's silence than she had going in, looked back at a face that seemed torn by some internal conflict raging just beyond her reach. Remembering that it was she who had instigated this surprise meeting and starting to realise that perhaps it had been a mistake, she resolved to be the first to speak.

"Mr Blake, I hope it's okay that I came here unannounced. It's just that you didn't leave a phone number with the marina and I need to talk to you about your ship that's still docked with us, and its cargo. Dub's back now. I don't know if you heard. Thanks to you, of course." She said the last part more quietly and, as she did so, Blake noticed the blood beginning to fill her delicate cheeks. "I also just wanted to thank you again for what you did. Everyone in town was asking about you, but I guess they've moved on to the next thing now that Dub's back and in one piece."

Though her words were polite, her look asked why she was being kept on the threshold instead of being invited in. Blake, interpreting her expression correctly and realising his own rudeness, broke his silence for the first time and replied, "It's quite alright, Ms Harrison. Please come in."

"Call me Ginny," she said, smiling as she stepped into the large atrium.

Once inside she looked around the small, circular room and asked, "So where have you been? It's a small town so I'd assumed that I would be seeing you around, only I never did."

Blake followed her back into the house and answered, "I've been here mostly, trying to get the house in order."

Still looking around, Ginny observed coquettishly, "And here I thought that all of your stuff was docked down at our marina!"

Blake allowed himself a small grin and answered, "No, not everything. Some items that I thought important to have on the crossing, yes, but not everything. Most of my furniture, at least the pieces that I wanted to keep, was shipped here and offloaded prior to my arrival so that I wouldn't have to arrive to an empty house, completely devoid of any familiarity."

She smiled again and stated with a finality that implied the subject was about to change, "Well, you have a lot of house to fill! I think it's very beautiful."

Ginny meant what she said and found herself overwhelmed by the beauty and antiquity of Blake's furniture. She yearned to see the rest of the house, for she knew that if an atrium could boast such beautiful décor, then the main rooms of the house would certainly be even more splendid. Turning again to Blake, she noticed the details of his face in the light of the bright atrium for the first time.

"Are you okay?" she asked, studying him with concern.

It was true that his visage had changed for the worse in the months since she had last seen him. He was paler than he had been before, and gaunt. His face had grown sallow and sunken, and his breathing seemed more laboured than it should have been under the circumstances.

"I'm very well, thank you. I just haven't had a chance to get out of the house lately."

She eyed him suspiciously but decided not press the issue and turned the conversation instead to business.

"So, about your cargo. Dub wanted me to come talk to you about it. He couldn't believe that it was still there when he got back and that I hadn't made you come and haul it off. He's mad because he says it makes his insurance premiums go up to keep it there. In short, it would make my life much easier if you would just arrange to have it offloaded and hauled somewhere else."

She concluded her plea and gave Blake a plaintive look. He smiled and answered that he would, of course, make the arrangements to have his cargo offloaded and moved to a new location right away.

-VI-

A FEW DAYS AFTER HER VISIT TO BLAKE'S MANOR, GINNY was sitting at her desk updating logs when she saw the pale-faced master of the house approaching from a nearby street.

She rose from her work and stood in her office doorway, calling out to him as he neared, "I assume you're here to keep your promise and finally unload your cargo? Dub's been a nightmare ever since he got back."

He looked up at her and answered evenly, still walking, "I am, Ms Harrison, just as promised."

He reached her door and the first thing she noticed was yet another stark change in his countenance. The face, while still pale, seemed fuller, less sunken and healthier. His breathing was steady and unlaboured, and he exuded strength and virility where before he had appeared weak and sickly. The drastic change struck her, but she endeavoured not to give herself away by allowing her look to linger too long.

"Come on in," she said, indicating to him the same chair facing her desk in which he had sat during their first meeting.

They both sat and went quickly through the remaining paperwork. By the end of their meeting it was established that a moving crew would arrive straight away in order to unburden the small marina of the unwelcome cargo and, with Blake's signature still glistening wet on a freshly printed slip lease, that the *Eugenia* would be staying docked right where it was for the foreseeable future. Only once during this meeting did the newly reinstated Dub poke his head in, and when he did, it was clear that he had not been expecting to find Ainsley Blake there. During their brief correspondence, Blake could tell that Dub was having an exceedingly difficult time keeping a lid on just how annoyed he'd truly been with the cargo that had so long overstayed its welcome, but also that the good-hearted, old man was doing everything in his power, out of respect for the man who had saved his life, to prevent himself from saying anything about it that might be in poor taste. When Dub left, Blake turned back to face Ginny with a look of amused perplexity.

"Told you," answered Ginny in reply to his expression. "I thought maybe his episode might have calmed him down a little, but he came back grumpier than ever." She leaned closer to him and went on in a whisper. "I think he's embarrassed. Dub's not the kind of guy that's used to needing a whole lot of help."

Blake cast a cursory glance over his shoulder and then looked again at Ginny and said seriously, "One does not like to be reminded that one is mortal."

Ginny nodded with deep comprehension and pitied Dub from then on. With the last of the paperwork signed, the cargo transfer initiated and the matter of the *Eugenia*'s mooring and maintenance settled, the two rose from their seats to say goodbye. As Blake turned to leave, Ginny stopped him suddenly.

"Listen. I know the other day you said you hadn't had a chance to get out much, so…" She paused nervously, second-guessing her courage, but soon persevered and went on. "I was thinking maybe I could show you around? If you want. What do you think?"

This caught Blake totally off guard and, as a result, he answered automatically from his heart before his reason could intervene.

"Yes, I would very much like that."

Instantly after answering, he recovered and cursed himself for his lack of self-control (he seemed to be doing a lot of that lately) but was still determined not to let on that he was now overflowing with regret so as not to hurt the poor girl's feelings.

Ginny, reacting quite the opposite way to Blake, smiled brightly and said, beaming, "Great! Why don't you meet me at Proust tomorrow morning at ten? It's my favourite coffee shop in town. You can't miss it, the town's so small and it's right on the main drag."

She looked at him sheepishly, thinking how small indeed the town must seem to a man who had crossed the Atlantic Ocean alone in his own sailboat.

Blake exhaled slowly and said, "I will be there," and then abruptly left the office.

Immediately after Dub had left the two young people alone in Ginny's office, he had quickly busied himself with scraping barnacles off of various boat propellers in order to quiet his thoughts. It was slow and tedious work, but Dub found that that was the best kind whenever he needed to brood. What he'd seen transpiring in his office had unnerved him, and whenever something beyond his own comprehension disturbed his peace he sought to immediately snuff it out with menial tasks. It was the way that Ginny looked at the new stranger that unsettled him. He had known her for a very long time and had never seen her nervous around anyone like today. She'd watched this Blake's face so carefully that Dub wasn't even sure that she had looked up at him at all when he'd poked his head in. It wasn't that the stranger was a bad man – he'd saved his life, after all – it was just that Dub always worried about Ginny. His worry was paternal in nature and was the inevitable consequence of any situation that he felt left her potentially vulnerable. The stranger could have been anyone and Dub would have felt exactly the same way. In theory, he had always wanted Ginny to find love and be happy, but now that he sensed it was actually within her grasp, he found that being happy for her, rather than sick with worry, was far more easily said than done.

After several hours, Dub, red-faced, exhausted and finding that the barnacles were doing little in the way of alleviating his concern all by themselves, decided to turn the radio on. Pivoting to face the ancient machine that had resided on the dock since the marina's earliest days, he swung the old, analogue channel dial onto the town's lone station. With the radio now playing, he returned to his barnacle-scraping as a voice he recognised from many years of monotonous reporting went over the day's news in an even tone.

"…it is, however, expected that both parties will make a full recovery. In other news, long-time town resident Jonathan Lange passed away last night peacefully as he slept. He was discovered in the early hours of this morning by an attending nurse responding to an alarm indicating that the sick man had gone into cardiac arrest. Despite numerous resuscitation attempts, Mr Lange was pronounced dead at the age of eighty-five. Mr Lange had no known living relatives and a rather large estate that is expected to be the subject of many a contentious debate in the coming weeks…"

Dub listened on absentmindedly, no longer scraping barnacles, long after the news had ended. As he looked out on to the water, a beautiful sunset painted the entire sky a bright, vivid red from horizon to horizon. Dub paused to take in the spectacle and as he drank in its intoxicating effects, he at long last felt his tranquillity return to him, washing away all of his previous worry.

When Hugo Wegener arrived at Blake's manor house that evening, he found a pensive Blake seated at their usual reading table, staring blankly at a far wall.

Hugo looked at him for a minute and then spoke. "You look rather lost in thought, my friend. Has something happened?" His friend did not respond and so Hugo, glancing down at an open newspaper that lay spread across the dark-red surface of the ancient walnut table, went on in a more casual tone. "Ah yes, what do you make of all this nonsense? When will people learn that greed is their main corruption and the inevitable vessel of their own downfall?"

The headline that displayed prominently on the open newspaper page read: *Lange Dead, Estate Uncertain.*

Still not drawing any sign of comprehension from Blake, he continued, "They've been talking about the unfortunate Mr Lange all over town. What do you make of it all? Is the man saint or sinner? The man unanimously hated by all, now supposed to be the most generous that the town has ever produced. I suspect there are some pretty ashamed people about town this evening. It's poetic, really, my friend, to have someone so good to be thought so evil and everyone to be proven so wrong."

This last part seemed to snap Blake out of his trance, and he looked up at Hugo and said quietly, "He was dying, Hugo. A condemned man."

"Ah," said Hugo, eyeing his friend and instantly understanding everything. "I see."

Blake went on with a pleading note in his voice. "It was a mercy. How could I have known?"

"You could not have, my friend. Mr Lange was not a beloved man nor a very open one. No one knew the nobility of his true intentions, nor could they have guessed the kindness of a heart so long buried in acrimony."

Blake considered Hugo's words seriously and slowly began to show small signs of relief. Sometimes the only thing needed to alleviate the immense pain of an offended conscience is the reassurance of a third party that the severity of one's actions does not warrant the harshness of the subsequent reproach. Feeling slightly less tormented, Blake reclined in his chair and said, "I suppose goodness will always make itself known in the end. The man lived a worthy life."

"Hear, hear," replied Hugo, taking a seat next to his friend at the antique table.

The two men sat together without saying much for a while. Both looked thoughtfully out of the dining-room window at a glorious sunset that turned the sky so vibrant a shade of red that the whole of heaven seemed set ablaze. As Blake stared into the beautiful colours, he was able to make peace with his own heart.

-VII-

A ROUND THE TIME THAT DUB WAS SCRAPING BARNACLES and Ainsley Blake was learning the truth about Jonathan Lange, Ginny was walking through town en route to her father's house. It seemed that the whole town was out and about, and every conversation was the same. Earlier in the day, they had all simultaneously been about what would become of the massive unclaimed fortune belonging to the recently departed Mr Lange. Now, their focus had shifted to the old man himself and how he could have been so misunderstood during the course of his life.

When the news had broken earlier that morning regarding the old man's death, the details of all subsequent legalities were poorly understood, and it had therefore been reported that there had been no heir designated in the will. This had ignited the imaginations of everyone in town and the whole place had been rife with speculation. This state of general chaos had lasted until lunchtime, when the local news channel announced that Mr Lange's lawyer was to issue a statement on the matter. The townspeople were so unanimously excited about the forthcoming statement that one might have thought NASA was preparing to announce the discovery of alien life. When the scrawny, bespectacled lawyer finally appeared at the media podium, the entire town had gone eerily quiet in anticipation. The lawyer looked nervous, but maintained himself and delivered his statement with as much professional integrity as anyone could have hoped for:

> *"Good afternoon, everyone. In accordance with the wishes of my late client, Mr Jonathan Lange, I wish to make a statement regarding the appropriation of the sizeable estate left behind by the departed. All worldly assets will immediately be transferred into a trust account for the benefit of the local community in the form of scholarships for qualifying residents wishing to attend college, and funding for the local arts and sciences. Further, a separate fund will be put into place to be used solely for the forgiveness of student loan debt for qualifying local college graduates. Lastly, several new treatment centres will be constructed in conjunction with the local medical clinic specialising in ailments both physical and mental. All arrangements have been made in accordance with the last will and testament of Mr Jonathan Lange. I will not take any questions at this time. Thank you very much for your attention."*

When the lawyer left, and the podium stood empty, the silence of the town persisted momentarily under the weight of what had just been said. Most were shocked that a man so universally disliked by every person in town could have, in the end, devoted his life's entire fortune towards helping the same. Some were ashamed at the beliefs they had maintained regarding the old man's character when he had been alive and regretted that they had not endeavoured to befriend him prior to his death. Others were deeply saddened that the old man had spent his final days alone and in a hospital. The rest, but this was by far the smallest group, saw only selfish opportunity in the statement that the lawyer had made, and thought only of how best to get their share of the fortune that had been given as a gift for the benefit of the entire town.

Ginny, dodging questions from excited neighbours as she strolled through town, did not fall into any of these categories. She had not known Mr Lange and therefore entertained no thought whatsoever about what was to become of his money now that he was gone. She had no right to it as far as she was concerned and nobody else did either. She had indeed been moved, as the rest of the town had, when the entirety of the dramatic story had finally broken and the full details had been divulged concerning the old man's sad end and the divinely altruistic action which he had undertaken in death. She had wept for him, as she wept always for things both beautiful or in pain, or, in cases like this, both. Walking down the street now, however, she was fully recovered and firmly resolved not to engage in the gossip that was threatening to consume the whole of the town. She walked purposefully, with her eyes focused directly in front of her, not daring to acknowledge even one of the numerous people that were attempting to draw an opinion out of her regarding the extraordinary saga of Jonathan Lange. Ginny thought amusedly about the town's constant need for fresh gossip and supposed it was the same in every small town. It was only a week ago that the whole town had been abuzz regarding the mysterious Ainsley Blake and his attempted murder of Dub, and now it was as if that had never even happened. She wondered to herself if they had all genuinely forgotten it.

Once through the main drag of town, where the Lange-enthusiasts were at their most dense, Ginny found herself largely unopposed in the remainder of her journey to her father's. She ducked through a back alley that she'd discovered as a shortcut in her youth and emerged mere yards from her father's immaculate house. Standing at his front door, she slammed the bronze knocker and heard the familiar shuffling sounds from inside grow louder with proximity until the heavy door swung open.

Her father beamed down at her with his youthful eyes. "Hello, sweetheart."

"Hi, Daddy!" she replied, smiling back up at him.

"Are you ready?" he asked.

"As ready as I'll ever be, I guess," said Ginny, and then added good-naturedly, "You know I secretly thought that if I didn't say anything you'd just forget about all this."

Her father smiled and guided her across the threshold, saying only, "Not this time, sweetheart."

He let her pass by him into the house and then gave the brilliant red sunset that had only just begun to spread its fiery reach across the sky one last look. He didn't know why, but it was the most beautiful sunset that he could ever remember having seen, and it seemed to take the many hardships and sins of his long life and wash them clean away. He closed his eyes and inhaled a deep breath before turning back into the house to rejoin his daughter and begin their work. Starting tonight they would turn the absurd dream of a zoo into a reality.

-VIII-

THE FOLLOWING MORNING, GINNY WAS SITTING IN PROUST flipping through a book, the title of which she had not even read, with her eyes fixed unblinkingly on the entrance through which she knew Blake must enter. Her heart raced and her palms were sweaty, both of which were sensations so alien to the happy girl that she did not even know to what exactly they should be attributed. She wiped her moist hands on the sides of her dress and tried again to read the book in front of her but found that she remained wholly unable to concentrate in the midst of her anxiety. Eventually, in a gesture of surrender to her nerves, she closed the thick volume and dropped it onto the table. Checking the time, she found, to her great annoyance, that it was still a quarter out from ten o'clock. Frustrated, and growing more antsy by the minute, she stood to refill her coffee, thinking to herself that caffeine was probably the last thing that someone in her condition needed, but also that she was lost as to any other means of passing the fifteen unbearable minutes that must first elapse before Blake would officially be late. As she stood at the counter filling her cup, she heard the bell ring behind her, indicating that someone had just entered the coffee shop. Her body tensed in expectation and she was unable to prevent herself from spilling a dash of hot coffee onto the soft skin of the back of her hand. She put it immediately to her mouth in order to ease the pain, and slowly turned to meet the dark eyes of Ainsley Blake. She had known that it was him even before she'd turned to face him. He was more than ten minutes early and she appreciated it. She detested worthless social conventions like being "fashionably late" but admitted to herself that she would have forgiven him immediately if he had been so. They stood looking at each other until Blake, noticing the hand at Ginny's mouth, broke the silence.

"Did you burn yourself?"

Ginny glanced down at her hand as if seeing it for the first time, and dropped it abruptly to her side, looking embarrassed. "Yes, I spilled some coffee on it."

Blake approached her and took the afflicted hand in his own, saying, "Let me see." He examined the reddened patch of agitated skin and then said to her, without dropping her hand, "I think you will live."

She smiled at him and found, much to her delight, that it was much easier to meet his eyes in the wake of this small joke. With the tension slightly eased, the pair sat down at Ginny's table. She picked up a menu, but Blake did not follow suit. Instead he stared fixedly across the table at her, showing no interest whatsoever in menus.

Following his lead, she put her menu down on the table and looked back at him, asking, "So what do you think of the place? I probably come here every day at least once. I keep trying to get them to name something on the menu after me but haven't had any luck so far."

"It is very nice," said Blake, taking a look around at the book-covered walls. "Almost like a library in itself. It is named for the French writer, is it not?"

"Yes, exactly. You may have noticed that the town has a slight obsession with all things French. Just don't ask them where their ancestors came from and you should be alright. Have you ever read any Proust?"

"Oh, yes," said Blake, still scanning the walls. "Many times."

Ginny looked back at him, thrilled and impressed. Aside from herself she did not know of anyone else in town that had, although most would undoubtedly claim otherwise.

Blake, finishing his scan of the walls, turned his gaze back to Ginny. "You are fond of literature then?"

At this, Ginny laughed so loud and abruptly that it ended in a snort and said, "Oh my God, it's my life. Being stuck here, it's the only way I can get to other places. I come here every day and read, sometimes for hours if it's quiet down at the marina."

Blake, listening intently, asked her seriously, "But you have not been to any other places?"

Ginny, caught slightly off guard by this direct question, looked down and answered him in a quieter voice. "I was going to travel but, well, it just never worked out. My dad is here, and then when Dub's wife got sick and I started helping out at the marina… it was supposed to be temporary, but it just kept going, and now I don't know how to go. Dub needs me here and now I'm starting to think my dad does to. He's just gotten this idea in his head that…"

She stopped talking, worried that she had been rambling, and looked up again at Blake with a slightly pleading expression. "You don't want to hear any of this."

Blake, however, assured her that he wanted very much to hear it and so she went on.

"Well, he's bought an old zoo." Seeing Blake's surprised look, she added quickly, "I know, I know, but hear me out. He and I always went to the zoo when I was a kid and I just worry that he's trying to hold on to something that isn't there. I think that he thinks that this is something that I would really want because I used to talk about how the animals could be treated better and was always telling him what I'd do if it were my zoo." Ginny paused and studied Blake's expression for a hint of what he might be thinking and then, unable to read his countenance, continued, "I know you think he's probably crazy, but I really don't think he is. If you saw him you'd see how young and strong he looks despite his age." Ginny leaned back with a contemplative look, and concluded, "I just think he wants to help. Help everyone. The community, the animals, me. I don't know, maybe he is going crazy."

She had half expected Blake to start laughing at her, but he never did.

Instead he said simply, "I don't think he's crazy. And if this zoo will bring him happiness then I don't think there is any reason to assume it is not the right thing to do."

This statement was not at all what Ginny had been expecting and she felt her heart swell with gratitude.

"I'm so glad that you think so," said the young girl with glistening eyes.

The next hour and a half were spent mainly in happy conversation regarding literature. Following the emotional confession of her father's mad plan, the two had silently agreed to digress to the lighter topic of the many books that decorated the walls at Proust. Ginny did most of the talking about her favourite authors and all of the books she loved, how her reading list was always growing because she added to it at a rate many times that at which she was able to read what was already on there, and the frustration of never having seen any of the wonderful cities in which all the stories she loved were set. Blake listened without adding much other than small questions overtly designed to keep her talking about herself. She noticed that he did not seem very keen to talk about his own life, but she yearned for him to because she could see a depth in his eyes that could only be the result of innumerable and varying experiences. She also could not forget that the reason they'd met in the first place was because he had crossed the Atlantic in a sailing vessel piloted only by himself. This alone merited at least some discussion over coffee. She decided not to press him for information, however, and contented herself happily talking about her own life, and those books which were her dearest passion. Blake listened until her voice began to grow hoarse with prolonged use and then got up from his chair, smiling, and, to her surprise, extended her a hand.

"Come on. I want to show you something."

Ginny took the outstretched hand, not knowing what to expect, and rose slowly from her seat. She felt herself growing nervous again as he led her out of the coffee shop and out onto the street, but the thought of not complying made her more nervous still. After they had walked a few blocks she chanced a question.

"So, where are we going?"

Blake smiled back at her, but when he saw the discomfort written across her delicate features, his smile faltered slightly.

"No need to be nervous, Ms Harrison. I just have something that I think you will very much enjoy seeing."

Ginny, reassured by the calming tone of Blake's voice, smiled again and answered with a smirk, "I told you to call me Ginny."

The two walked on and discussed trivial matters in a light-hearted manner more like that which had prevailed at the coffee shop. Ginny told Blake about her hometown in sweeping generalities that he guessed could probably apply to any small American town, and he told her about the busy streets of London that were so different, careful to avoid divulging anything of substance about himself personally. When the inevitable topic of Jonathan Lange came up, Blake remembered the peace he had been given in the spectacular sunset that had assuaged his guilt and found, to his surprise, that he encountered no trouble in discussing it. Of course, the two were only discussing it in adherence to the town's unanimous decision that it must be discussed, and so did not assign to it any real severity that might have made the prospect more difficult. By the time they reached the periphery of the town's main drag, Ginny began to suspect that they were heading to Blake's manor house. A few more minutes' walk soon confirmed that suspicion when they arrived at the ornate gates to the property and Blake swung them open to admit her.

Once Ginny had entered the grounds, Blake followed behind her, careful to leave the gate ajar so as not to give her the impression of being trapped. However, despite this precaution, Ginny showed no signs of her previous nervousness now that they had arrived at the manor house. On the contrary, she seemed quite cheerful. Far from thinking herself in any danger, she was busy in deep speculation about the contents of the manor house that she was certain she had been brought there to see and, remembering the grandeur of the atrium, her expectations were high. Blake noticed the youthful cheerfulness that had overtaken the delighted girl and felt once again his old heart lurch.

Ginny turned to look at him with a slightly flushed face and said, "So, what did you want to show me?"

Blake walked straight past her, saying, "Come with me."

Ginny, not daring now to disobey, followed him through the front door and back once more into the glorious atrium.

Once through the atrium, Ginny followed Blake into a dining room that held an extraordinary dining table of dark wood almost completely obscured by large and old-looking books. He did not stop there, however, and, beckoning her to follow, continued on into another room before she had even had a chance to fully appreciate that which they were leaving. This process of entering and immediately exiting rooms continued through several more of the home's many chambers, despite the fact that each contained innumerable pieces of magnificent furniture that Ginny was desperate to examine in more depth, until they emerged at last into what was easily the largest room that they had so far entered. The second Ginny's eyes were able to acclimate to the darker light, she knew that they had reached the room which Blake had longed for her to see. Every wall was covered with thick, highly polished wooden shelves and on every shelf rested countless books that ranged in size from what Ginny thought must be paper throwaways, to enormous, leather-bound and ancient-looking tomes of unknown origin and composition. She was speechless and Blake did not say anything as he allowed the vast contents of the library to wash over her.

After a few minutes of staring aghast around at the walls, Ginny managed to say in a staggered voice, "How... where... I mean, how did you... where did you get all these?"

Blake smiled at her and answered serenely, "This library has been in the possession of my family for hundreds of years and we've been accumulating books throughout that entire time. Among its thousands of volumes are unpublished works by some of literature's greatest and most influential, as well as personal notebooks, letters and items of a similar nature. And, of course, more traditionally known novels, as well as professional and scientific treatises."

Blake watched her for a few minutes as she absorbed her surroundings, wanting her to appreciate it as much as he had believed that she would. Once he had contented himself with her reaction, he ran a steady hand over the spines of several books on the lowest shelf until he seemed to locate what it was he was looking for, and then stopped. He carefully extracted an old-looking volume with a bright-red cover and gold pages that appeared to be only the first of a multi-volume set, and opened it to the title page.

He held it out to Ginny and said, "Here. This is what I wanted to show you."

Ginny, far too nervous to accept the ancient-looking book, resisted, but with Blake's insistence, carefully took the aged piece of literature in her hands and read:

Middlemarch
A Study of Provincial Life
By:
George Eliot
Vol. I

Ginny gasped as soon as she had read it and nearly dropped the precious tome. Thankfully, however, she recovered herself, knowing that to drop something so priceless would be a sin against the world and refusing to commit it. Once she had regained her composure, she looked at Blake with watering eyes.

Blake looked gently back at her and said, pointing down at the book, "Look below the title."

Ginny turned her gaze back down to the open page in front of her and let out a shriek that showed just how truly overwhelmed she had become, as she read the following inscription, hand-written delicately below the title in a dark ink:

My dearest Ainsley,

Though your position has been made clear, and I dare not contest your avow as to what it is your heart desires, I hope that some perspective can be gained herein and that one day, here in our real world, Miss Brooke may indeed find her Will Ladislaw.

With love now and always,
MAE
20th June 1871

It seemed that the hand-written inscription was the final straw, and Ginny, no longer able to keep herself upright under the weight of her emotion, sank onto trembling knees.

Blake, being for many years unaccustomed to the effect that strong emotion can produce on susceptible people, became alarmed and kneeled quickly down to her level. Closing the book and putting it aside, he asked softly, "Are you alright? After what you told me at the coffee shop I thought that you might enjoy seeing that. I see now that it was mistake and I sincerely apologise."

Blake continued looking at her face in silence, second-guessing his choice of words, as Ginny gave him a confused look that said in no uncertain terms that he had egregiously misinterpreted the nature of her reaction.

In a tone more resilient and defiant than he had expected, Ginny replied to his enquiry. "A mistake? How could you say that? This is one of the most wonderful things I have ever seen. I don't know how I will ever thank you for showing me this. I don't even know how to process it." She looked around, shaking her head and struggling to find words capable of properly conveying feelings that were beyond the scope of human language. After a few more moments spent in fruitless searching, she gave it up and moved on to a more easily attainable aspiration, saying, "The inscription. It was to Ainsley. Is that supposed to be some sort of coincidence, or is it a joke? Or someone in your family? How did you get this?"

Blake, looking only slightly unnerved as if he had feared this question but was ready for it, answered as calmly as he could. "Yes, someone in my family. The Ainsley to which this inscription was written was my third great-grandfather on my father's side. He…" Blake paused, as if reminiscing, and then went on with emotion that he was clearly trying to conceal. "He knew Ms Evans on a very personal level, as I'm sure you could tell from the inscription. He – my grandfather, I mean – could not carry on the relationship, however, and they parted ways. Nine years later she was dead and it impacted him terribly. He always felt that he had had no choice in the matter and that, despite his pain, he acted in accordance with his conscience."

Blake stood and turned away from Ginny to look out of a nearby window, but she could see the pain clearly marked in the features he was attempting to hide from her. She felt a surge of pity, gratitude and warmth towards him rise within her, and, without a clear idea of what it was that she intended to do, she stood herself up and approached the window.

Blake did not look back immediately, but when he felt the soft, gentle hand touch his shoulder, he turned to find himself kissing the woman who had been the object of his affection ever since he had first seen her that night at a movie theatre. She had been his desire, his fear, his pain, his reminder of past mistakes, his warning of mistakes still to come and now, in his arms, she was his only hope. She was his saviour or she was his destroyer, and he knew with absolute truth that he would follow her to either end.

He embraced her still more tightly, knowing what it might mean, and the repressed passion of lifetimes rose from the abyss inside of him, boiling over and into Ginny. He dispelled with his reason which would surely protest, and his conscience which would certainly forbid, and he held her, never wanting to let go. His heart, so long oppressed, throbbed in defiance, and his body tingled. He had known that she was dangerous and now he surrendered to her, and he would surrender to her again and again as many times as she wanted. Each of them became the other's and they both accepted it as what they had both wanted since the beginning. They stood, entangled for what seemed like an eternity, not daring to let go. Because a first kiss is no guarantee of a second, and they both wanted to postpone the separation so as to longer savour the glory. When the two finally did separate, Ginny, nervous and a little embarrassed by her own rashness, looked up at Blake's face with a smile, and when she found that he too was smiling, her misgivings melted away and all that was left was happiness.

In the days that followed, Ainsley Blake and Virginia Harrison were inseparable. Aside from her work at the marina, and a vexatious need for sleep each night, they spent almost all available time together. She basked in his knowledge and the resources of his library, and he revelled in the happiness that he had never expected to be given again. Her mind was keen and she absorbed information at a feverish pace that Blake could not help but be impressed with.

He spent hours with her discussing the various books she had read from his shelves and the true histories of the periods during which they were set. His insights allowed her to perceive the connections between her favourite stories and the conditions in reality that had given rise to them. She drew her own inspiration from the sources of their inspirations and dove back into their worlds at every interval during which she was not otherwise engaged. She spent so much time poring over the volumes that comprised Blake's vast collection that she was completely devoid of any considerations regarding those who might have existed in Blake's life prior to her arrival. She had, without realising it, defaulted to the assumption that he was alone in life. It wasn't just because that was the feeling she got, but also because he had only just recently arrived in town and the necessary time during which one might acquire any intimate connections had simply not yet elapsed. In selfish and blissful ignorance, she sat each day, lost in ancient pages, happily unaware of a certain disgruntled doctor who had been displaced in the wake of her arrival.

-IX-

Dr Hugo Wegener sat at Ainsley Blake's ornate dining table pretending to read, while in reality thinking with concern about his own recent demotion in the hierarchy of Blake's growing social circle. He only came here a few times a week now, and for only a few hours at a time, when "that girl", as he liked to call her, was off working at the marina. He thumbed the pages of the unread book in front of him irritably as he thought, and then finally concluded that he must bring his concerns up with his friend rather than leave them to continue developing unimpeded within himself. The good doctor, understandably not excited about this potentially unpleasant encounter, but still convinced as to its necessity, shored up his decision by reminding himself that his motives were unselfish, and that it was actually his duty as a friend to intervene in their blossoming romance before it was too late. Hugo did not have to wait long for his chance. Immediately after he had formed his resolution, he heard the familiar footsteps of his friend approach the dining room from some distant chamber, and it wasn't long before the master of the house entered the very room in which a nervous Hugo Wegener had been giving a secret audience to his own tormented thoughts. Blake walked in without looking up from the book that was in his hand and it was clear from the first glance that he was as untroubled and focused as Hugo was the opposite. Hugo watched him for a while in silence before finally summoning the courage necessary to bring up what it was that he wished to discuss and, when at last he found his voice, observed that it was slightly softer and more timid than he had intended.

"I say, Blake. Do you think it's wise for you to be spending so much time with this girl?"

Blake looked up from his book and into his friend's eyes. His initial expression was one of surprise, but it quickly faded into melancholy as he said, "No, I do not think it is wise." His head dropped slightly and he let the book in his hand fall at his side. "Surely you know that I tried not to... that I did everything I could?"

Hugo looked back at his friend, this time with sympathetic eyes that had been softened by Blake's immediate surrender. Inwardly, he was enormously surprised and greatly relieved that Blake had put up so little fight. The doctor had been preparing himself mentally, and not without considerable anxiety, for a drawn-out confrontation during which he would have to argue the rationality of his position with a man consumed by the irrationality of love's madness.

"Yes, my friend. I do, of course. But now it's time to end it. Surely you understand that?"

Hugo spoke softly and walked over to Blake, who was now hunched with his hands on the windowsill, and placed a consoling hand on his shoulder.

Blake looked up at him with an expression that was both defiant and confused, and said, "End it?"

Hugo, clearly not expecting this response and preparing himself again for the confrontation that he thought he'd managed to avoid, removed his hand from Blake's shoulder and took a step back. "Well, yes. You know as well as I the risks involved here. Not just to us, but to her as well. Perhaps especially to her. Why, we just discussed this a few weeks ago, my friend. Surely you remember? Surely you know that it is madness?"

Blake, still not taking his eyes off Hugo, rose and stood tall and steady.

Turning from the windowsill and taking a step towards his retreating friend, he said with a rising voice, "And what would the good doctor have me do? Live out this cursed existence alone and in constant retreat from a danger that I am doomed to face regardless? Shall I hide and push her away, as I have done with others for countless years? Exiling myself and my heart? Do I, do we, not have a right to the happiness taken for granted by so many undeserving, mortal men?"

Blake's voice kept rising higher as he spoke and he continued involuntarily taking threatening steps towards the small man who, in turn, matched Blake's strides in reverse so as to maintain the distance between them. Noticing the retreat and seeing the fearful expression written across his friend's face, Blake realised with shame that intimidating a being whose intentions were apparently pure was a sin more in line with the past to which he had vowed long ago never to return. So, regaining his self-control with effort, he quickly halted his advance and attempted to soften his features. Even now, however, wearing an expression that struggled to reflect a placidity that was not present, it was apparent that Blake was finding it exceedingly difficult to maintain mastery over his anger.

When at last he had gained some semblance of control, he looked, trembling, at Hugo and said in a tone more defeated than anything else, "I cannot stop, Hugo. I could not stop even if I tried. You know as well as I that love cannot be put aside or persuaded. To attempt to contain a force so powerful is to try to stop the movements of the heavens. And, for men who try, at the end there is only madness and despair."

Hugo bowed his head in acknowledgment of the fruitlessness

of continued opposition, and said, "You have made your choice then. So be it. However, I cannot be a part of it. You risk your exposure and along with it, my own. You risk the girl and her family, and I will not be party to it."

At this, the look of anger that Blake had been just barely managing to contain began to resurface on his face, and he snapped back suddenly and ferociously at the subdued doctor.

"So, that's it then? You will leave? I forgot that the honour of the noble Hugo Wegener extended beyond his own fleeting appetites. What of the family of the glutinous and perverse, but still innocent, Obadiah Davids? Was he not deserving of your mercy? And now you abandon me, too? After so many years alone and wandering, you will leave it all?"

Blake was panting with anger, but it was the kind of anger that exists only as a mask. A mask designed so that one might not be made to reveal the vulnerability they so desperately want to conceal in the face of someone who has dealt them a great blow to the heart. Hugo did not respond immediately but gave Blake a pitying look that showed he understood the true origin of his rage.

After a few minutes of heavy silence, Hugo spoke again, softly but with unmistakable finality. "I understand your anger, Ainsley, but I cannot stay."

Blake, recognising that he had lost and unable to offer a single rational argument in favour of his own behaviour, collapsed into an armchair in the corner of the room with his face buried in his hands.

Hugo approached him sympathetically and placed a hand once again on his friend's shoulder. "I truly wish you success, my friend. I mean that absolutely and with all my heart. And perhaps we may meet again someday."

With these last words, Hugo left the room and, a moment later, Blake heard the heavy front door open and then close with a thud. All was still now and he knew that his friend was gone.

The next few hours were some of the loneliest that Blake had ever suffered. Though he had spent the bulk of his many years in solitude, he had become accustomed to the company of the eccentric Hugo Wegener and now, though the good doctor had only just left, he felt his absence weighing down upon him and isolating him more than ever. Without realising it, and even before Ginny Harrison had broken through his most obvious defences, he had dropped his guard just enough to allow his new friend to penetrate to a depth of his heart that had remained undisturbed for many years previous. Now, the open wound in his heart that had been pricked first by Hugo, and then torn wide by Ginny, throbbed in agony with the absence of the former, and he knew that his only solace lay in the latter. He hoped that her love would be such that it would fill the whole of his heart and, if it was, then perhaps one day the memories of Dr Hugo Wegener could be recalled with fondness rather than pain.

Across town in an immaculately kept house, at the same moment Blake was contemplating the unexpected rupture of his friendship with Hugo, Ginny sat with her father poring over numerous documents regarding the upcoming renovation of the insane zoo. The pair had been steadily at work since earlier that morning when Dub had unexpectedly given Ginny the day off to spend with her family. It seemed that ever since his brush with death, Dub had become extremely concerned that Ginny was not seeing enough of her father and, consequently, she found herself with more days off now than she'd had in years. Although she worried about leaving Dub alone at the docks, she always accepted graciously and with abundant gratitude, feeling that to reject the offer might upset the old man. She attributed the change in his attitude not only to fresh considerations of his own mortality but also to feelings that she thought must have been awakened in him regarding his beloved wife, whom he had been unable to comfort in her final hours. Ginny knew that the fishing trip that had been the cause of his absence at the bedside of his dying wife had always haunted him, though he never spoke of it. By accepting Dub's offer, she thought she might in some way be easing the secret burden of the old man's suffering. Her suspicion as to Dub's true motive in offering her time off was so strong, in fact, and so sacred to her, that she dared not use that time off in the way she truly desired and run straight back into the waiting arms of her Ainsley Blake. Feeling that it would be an insult to the late Mrs Dobbs and a betrayal of the living Dub, she spent these days instead with her loving father, in accordance with Dub's wishes, and in service to the absurd zoo.

The goal of today's work was to officially procure the services of the contractors that would be needed to do the highly specialised type of labour required by a property whose sole purpose was to contain and nourish things not meant to be contained or nourished by men. Ginny's first priority in the screening process had initially been price until her father had overruled in favour of quality, arguing that when matters of life are concerned, doing it correctly as opposed to cheaply was a moral obligation that was to be abided without question.

Fortunately, and to Ginny's great surprise, her father had shown himself to be an extraordinarily capable businessman. When he had initially purchased the decaying zoo it had, not surprisingly, come with a litany of woefully complacent employees whose sole task it was to care for the zoo's existing animal population, as it had been even in the zoo's former glory days.

A quick glance at the zoo's meagre balance sheet by Ginny, who was familiar with such financial reports thanks to her job at the marina, showed that an unchecked trickle of state funds had somehow allowed these employees to continue collecting their pay cheques uninterrupted throughout the zoo's long decline and miraculously, the money still flowed even now after the deed was signed and ownership officially transferred from the city to its new private owner.

Although the state funds clearly appeared to be an overlooked line-item from a budget compiled during a long-lost time when the zoo still served its primary purpose as a source of education and family-friendly fun for the public, Ginny's father did not feel an immediate need to alert any officials at the state level of their apparent oversight. It seemed to him that the money was necessary to keep the animals in good health, and that without it they would have long ago been removed from the premises and scattered across the country's various other facilities.

The thought of the animals' well-being, and the necessity of keeping them where they were so that the community could once again enjoy them, was enough for the old man to maintain that he was in possession of the moral high ground, and that his silence to the state was justified. The old man further surprised his daughter when he announced one morning that his petition for membership, which she had had no idea he was even pursuing, in the Association of Zoos and Aquariums, or AZA, as it was commonly referred to, had been accepted, and that they would be receiving federal funding in addition to the trickle of state funds that they had been solely relying upon up to that point.

With the addition of the new funds, the inexplicably wise, first-time businessman immediately gave an organisation-wide pay increase in the amount of five per cent as his first order of business. When the employees, who could not remember when they had last received a pay raise, got the news, a new breath of life swept through the whole of the decrepit zoo and, to the great surprise of even the old man, the zoo began to revitalise itself of its own accord almost as if by magic.

At first, Ginny and her father noticed small changes. Sidewalks would be swept, lawns mowed, and trash collected and placed into bins. Over the next few weeks larger things began to happen. Fences and signs were sanded and repainted, and metal was scrubbed and polished. It was in the face of these changes and others that Ginny at long last abandoned her conviction that the wretched zoo had been but a passing fancy for the old man and recommitted herself entirely to the promise she had made to help in every way possible in order to make the dream into a reality.

Though Ginny had indeed resolved truthfully in her heart to apply herself completely to the project of the zoo, her dedication was admittedly lacking in practice. Although she spent each spare moment that Dub gifted to her with her father, she spent almost all others in the company of a man whom she still hardly knew. During the evening hours, when her mind was idle, she thought often about this. The persistent thought that kept her awake each night was made even more intrusive by her inability to deny to herself the growing power that the near-stranger had over her heart. She considered with anxiety her growing infatuation with the mysterious Blake but dared not to call it love. She wished that she could assure herself that she had maintained at least some level of control, but she knew that it was not the truth. Prematurely and against all logic, she had resigned herself completely to this man, and it was therefore in his sole power to complete or destroy her. And though, especially in consideration of the vulnerable position in which she currently found herself, she had every reason to be afraid, she was surprised to find that she instead felt only happiness.

Even the anxieties that tormented her at night were not born out of the fear of something terrible, but rather those one might experience in anticipation of some great adventure from which one returns a better and more complete version of themselves, having gained a valuable insight into the hidden purpose of life. It was not into the abyss that she walked but into the light, and one cannot travel in the presence of such lofty power without a corresponding physical response. Virginia Harrison was not just walking but sprinting into the light and she was doing so, as she did with everything, with her eyes wide open and full of wonder.

As Ginny sat in her father's house, flipping through a long list of contractors whose specialty happened to be water enclosures, she took no notice of the man himself who was sitting, quietly pretending to peruse his own lists, but in reality watching her carefully from across the room. The fact that there had been an abrupt and heretofore unexplained decline in the frequency of his daughter's visits had not been lost on the keen old man, and his curiosity was beginning to win out over his determination to respect his daughter's privacy. He glanced down one more time at the large binder in his hands containing the innumerable recommendations of contractors specialising in all things zoo that had been provided to them by the AZA, then, surrendering at last to his inability to concentrate, closed it with a loud thud and let it drop heavily onto the desk in front of him. The clap of the large binder hitting the desk made Ginny jump and she looked at her father surprised before collapsing almost immediately into laughter. He smiled involuntarily back at her as he always did whenever she laughed.

When she finally caught her breath, she exclaimed with unrestrained frivolity, "You scared me! What did you drop that huge thing for? You almost gave me a heart attack!"

Still smiling, he answered matter-of-factly, "Sorry. Didn't mean to drop it so noisily."

Ginny glared back at her father sarcastically, obviously suppressing a smile, and then turned her gaze back to the endless list at hand. Her father did not return to his binder but instead continued looking concernedly at his daughter, apparently struggling to ascertain the best approach in bringing up a subject of potential danger.

Clearing his throat nervously, he finally managed to say, "You know, sweetheart. It seems like I haven't been seeing as much of you lately. Is there anything that you want to tell me?"

Ginny looked up once more from her list, this time wearing an expression that showed she had not anticipated this question.

She looked quickly back down, at her hands this time instead of the list, and said with a hint of embarrassment, "Oh. Yeah, I know I haven't been around as much lately. It's just…" She trailed off, but her father, leaning forward with interest and concern, urged her on. "Well, I met someone."

With this admission, she looked back up at her father's face and held his gaze. In her eyes he could see how desperately she longed for his approval in this unprecedented matter of the heart, and he was determined to give it to her.

He smiled serenely at her and said in a comforting voice, "But why would you feel afraid to tell me that? You know I have wanted nothing more for you than your happiness."

Ginny, encouraged by this response, gave her father a smile of such authentic gratitude that it at once conveyed more appreciation than a million spoken "thank you"s could.

Her father, registering the effect that had been produced in his daughter and determining to hold on to it as long as possible, continued, "So, who is he? Is he here in town? Do I know him?"

As she thought about where to begin, he waited for her answer with genuine interest borne of a father's love. Ginny, still smiling broadly and seeming to have finally found the story's appropriate starting point, began again in an excited voice that was no longer embarrassed.

"Actually, Dad. He's one of the guys that we saw at the movie theatre that night a while ago. Do you remember? When we saw the rom-com? I thought you were staring at him and you told me that they were probably just from out of town? Anyway, you were certainly right about that part."

Ginny recounted the tale happily to her father, totally unaware that his countenance had completely shifted from one of optimistic curiosity to that of shock and fear. When she had at last concluded her tale, she sat pink-faced, having become excited in the midst of her recollections, and waited for her father to say something.

After a few more minutes of perplexing silence she started to worry again, and prodded. "Dad? Aren't you going to say anything?"

Her father, however, did not hear her, for inside his own head an epic battle was raging. On one hand, he did not approve of his daughter's new love interest, but on the other, he did not want to risk pushing her away by taking an overly hard line against the prospect. He had certainly lived long enough to know beyond the shadow of any doubt that a young girl in the clutches of a newly budding love will choose her lover over a disapproving father any day of the week. Fortunately, the vast wisdom acquired over the old man's many years had long ago endowed him with the ability to master his own emotions, and not allow them to cloud his perception as to what the most prudent course of action might be in a situation that carried with it a risk of great personal loss. This cherished ability, never present in the young, can be born only from first-hand experiences of tragedy brought upon by rash action, and mastered as those experiences multiply, until one's reason can finally gain mastery over the emotions that threaten it. Ginny's father had learned this lesson many times before and he used it to his advantage now.

Coming back to his full senses in the wake of his shock and subsequent musings, and realising quickly that his prolonged silence on the matter was jeopardising his newfound resolution not to upset his daughter, he forced a smile that he hoped would dispel her suspicion of his disapproval.

To his great relief, it appeared to have the desired effect when she smiled weakly back at him and asked shyly, "Are you mad?"

To this he gave her a look of deepest sympathy and replied, "Am I mad? Of course I'm not mad, sweetheart."

In an effort to appear more genuine, the old man rose from his seat and crossed the room to put a comforting hand on his daughter's shoulder before he went on.

"Like I said, I only want your happiness. And I would do anything to help you gain it. How could I possibly be mad if you tell me that you may have found it?"

Ginny smiled graciously up at him and said, "Thank you, Daddy."

The two remained in silence for a few more moments until the old man turned briskly and, clapping his hands together in an attempt to lighten the mood, said, "Well. I am going to want to meet this fellow! When can we all get together? I'd like to meet the man that is so worthy as to have finally moved your heart."

Ginny, with her spirits now fully restored, stood and immediately trapped her father in a rib-splitting hug. He hugged her back with his heart full of dread and, since she could not see, allowed it to flitter visibly across the features of his face for the briefest of instances. When they pulled apart his expression was once again jovial and he beamed down at his daughter, who returned his expression.

"I love you, Daddy," she exclaimed, and then turned and hurried towards the door with no other thought in her head but that of returning to Ainsley Blake with the welcome news that her father wanted to meet him.

She was only a few steps from freedom when her father called after her, "And where do you think you're going?"

Ginny stopped dead in her tracks and turned back to him with a look that was recognisable to her father as that which she had always worn as a young girl whenever she had been discovered doing something against the rules.

"I thought you wanted to meet him," she said, shrugging her shoulders.

"And I do. But I think that can wait for now, don't you? I didn't mean right this second!" He looked at her, really smiling now, and went on. "We still have work to do, and lots of it! Remember our deal, Ginny. You need to help me with the zoo. Even if there is a new man in your life. I don't want you getting too distracted and forgetting what we are trying to do here." He picked up the list of contractors that she had let fall onto the floor beside her empty chair and held it out to her, wearing a paternal look of authority that he knew she would be powerless against. "Now, where were we?"

Ginny begrudgingly took the list from his outstretched hand and, rolling her eyes, said, "Water enclosures."

While Ginny and her father talked on about water enclosures, they were not aware that more than four thousand miles away from where they sat, malicious forces were beginning to conspire against them within the dark veil of a dense jungle.

-X-

TIM FISCHER LIT HIS SECOND CIGARETTE OFF OF THE FIRST and then reclined at the bow of his small skiff as it headed out of camp a few miles inland from where the mighty Amazon met the Atlantic. He was just arriving back from a trip to Rio, where he had spent a few days with his mother, who had been in town visiting from the States.

Tim had been in Brazil just over a year now and his mom had shown during that period that she could be counted upon to visit him at least once a quarter, even more when he allowed it. He rarely did, however, because he found that the moment she departed again for home, it always left him wallowing in a state of profound uneasiness and shame. He loved her, certainly, but he hated seeing her. Of course, his mother, a sweet and deeply trusting woman from the Deep South, still believed her son to be enrolled in a study abroad programme through Georgia State University, which is what had originally brought about his long sojourn in South America. The truth of the matter was that Tim had dropped out of that programme after a mere three months in country. It seemed that living in the housing provided by the university, located in hip Ipanema, had proved too much for the sheltered young man, and it wasn't long before his new surroundings and accompanying freedom had succeeded in diverting his focus entirely away from his studies. By the three-month mark, Tim had fallen so far behind in the anthropology courses he had been undertaking while abroad that the situation had grown well beyond any hope of recovering. For most people, this failure would have meant an apologetic phone call to a parent and an immediate return flight home so that one might face the music and hope for sympathy, but for Tim this was not an option.

His mother, Dolores, had raised him as a single mom and had worked her hands into early arthritis years before it was naturally due her just so Tim could go to college and emerge on the other side debt-free. Now he had squandered a full semester abroad and spat at her great gift. In the immediate aftermath of this humiliating revelation, he vowed in earnest to make it right and set his mind to the task straight away.

He knew with certainty that withdrawing his enrolment in the university would mean an eviction from his student housing and so, assuring himself that this final misdeed was in service to his great forthcoming absolution, Tim cleverly amended the contact information in his college file to his own name, ensuring that any returned tuition from his unfinished classes would be furnished directly to him rather than the parent who had originally paid it. Once this dishonest act had been completed, he swore adamantly to himself that as soon as he had the money in hand, he would put it to use in righting the many wrongs he had committed against his dear and long-suffering mother.

Of course, things hadn't exactly worked out the way he had planned over the next few months and it didn't take long before Tim had run clean out of his meagre tuition refund. Penniless and threatened with the possibility of being hurled out onto the mean streets of Rio, he had been forced to borrow funds from the sort whom he would have been wiser to avoid. Through it all, however, the naïve and hopelessly optimistic Tim never forgot to remind himself that his redemption was right around the corner, and that these steps in the wrong direction were all temporary, completely reversible and absolutely necessary in achieving his greater goal of fixing everything before anyone back home ever found out it was broken. Unfortunately, after another month of no gains realised, the lenders had come looking for their money. With no hand left to play, Tim had been forced to throw himself at the mercy of the men to whom he was in debt, and whatever they needed, he would have no choice but to comply.

Tim took another long drag of his cigarette and gazed out over the banks of the river. Nothing there now except for dense jungle, completely untouched by humanity. Pure and serene. A charade that hid the dangers that lurked just beyond the thick veil of the tree line. Tim considered its beauty, and its secrets, and then thought back again to his time in Rio. Seeing his mother always brought the full gravity of his situation back to him and made it impossible for him to reconcile all of the mistakes he had made that had led him to his current predicament. Self-denial was his greatest ally and his mother's presence never failed to rob him of its comfort.

It turned out that when those men to whom he owed money had at last come to collect, and he had had no money with which to repay them, Tim had been forced to place himself in their service instead. Though their criminal portfolios were diverse, the men had, in the end, decided that Tim would be of greatest use out in the Amazon, in service to the bustling illegal animal trade that went on beneath the shadow of the great forest. Ever since, he had been chipping away at his considerable debt little by little, capturing rare species that were then smuggled out and sold off to the highest bidder. Every single time it made him sick. He loved animals and hated himself for what he was doing to them. After each one, he consoled himself with the belief that he didn't have a choice, and that one day he would make it all right again.

Tim flicked his cigarette into the belly of the enormous river and pushed the uncomfortable thoughts out of his mind. This was exactly why he hated it when his mother came to see him. It forced him to confront his own role in the deplorable fate that had befallen him. He readjusted himself at the bow of the small boat and then smiled slightly to himself, glancing down to the backpack at his side. There had been one thing about his mother's most recent visit that might actually make the whole thing worthwhile. She had brought with her, as she always did, a copy of their local hometown newspaper in order to show Tim what was going on back home. This was a ritual which she never failed to perform. He always suspected that her motive was to inspire homesickness and ultimately procure a commitment from him to return home, but what she didn't know was that Tim would give anything to come home and leave this place forever. He had perused the paper disinterestedly at first just to humour his mother, until a certain article had caught his eye. The article related the story of the old local zoo which had been purchased by a private third party and was soon to be refurbished. It had gone on to marvel at the incredible diversity of species it contained, as well as the decaying integrity of its ancient walls, which had miraculously remained upright despite many years of neglect.

Tim couldn't remember the zoo, but he certainly recognised an opportunity when he saw one.

The sun was beginning to set now as Tim's skiff puttered down the massive river. He checked the backpack periodically to make sure that the newspaper contained within was not being damaged by spray from the river. He needed it to last until he reached his destination. His boss, a burly, dangerous man originally from South Africa, had a camp just a few more miles downriver, and Tim was salivating at the opportunity to present this piece of information to him. He had always been terrified of his boss and even now, he felt that fear welling up inside himself as he drew near. His boss was someone whom Tim felt was completely devoid of good. A person robbed over time of any and all redeemable qualities. A man who could kill you or shake your hand at a whim.

When the skiff hit the bank of the river, Tim hopped out clutching the backpack like it was his child. He said a quick prayer in his head to a deity in which he did not believe and then made his way into the camp with hope in his heart that his liberty might finally be at hand.

-XI-

Later that night, while Tim Fischer was planting an immoral seed that would soon grow across continents, Ainsley Blake reclined in his library, gazing absentmindedly out the window into a dark sky. It was not on current happenings that he mused, but on those having transpired long ago in deep antiquity, though they still haunted him today. In his mind, he was not seated in a stately manor house on the East Coast of the United States, but in a world where the United States did not yet exist at all. Ainsley Blake, surrendering now completely to his memories, found himself content and untroubled in his mind's eye, basking in the warm glow of a fire that burned out many years ago, in a chamber with thick walls made from large stones.

He was lounging in a superb plush armchair of some great craftsmanship, periodically turning his head towards a large wooden door which served as the room's sole point of ingress or egress. He was expecting someone and was impatient with excitement at the prospect. Glancing around the room at the banners on the wall, his gaze fell upon a handsome crest that bore a red square shot through on all sides by thick red bars with the name "Blake" inscribed beneath it in a well-practised hand. He looked often at this crest because it was that of his father, and his father's father, and, as the present head of the house, he was determined to bring honour to it as had those who had come before him.

Of course, his predecessors had been gone for many years now and the lonely house of Blake had undoubtedly stagnated during a long period of conspicuous inactivity for which the history books would never be able to account. It was certainly not that there had been no activity at all, but that the activity that did occur in that lonesome house was always of a dark and secretive nature.

And though it was true that no transgression had been discovered yet by which the noble house's name might fall in standing, transgressions, and many, had indeed been committed by its mysterious master, in spite of his efforts to control himself, and the surrounding area was rife with suspicion.

More recently, however, life had stirred anew in the solitary house of Blake, and its reclusive patriarch had suddenly found himself at the mercy of feelings that rendered his sequestration a condition for which a remedy was immediately desirable. Tonight, he waited impatiently for that remedy to enter his chamber.

He had met her one evening while he was out riding in the countryside on the edges of his vast estate. Blake had ventured out under the cover of darkness in order to visit a plague-ravaged village that rested just beyond his own lands, which had recently been quarantined by the local government in an attempt to prevent the spread of the disease to neighbouring towns.

The dreadful state of the village was immediately perceptible when Blake entered. Everywhere he looked there were dead and dying. Half-dead men, women and children crawled towards unknown destinations that they would never reach, and that did not exist, with glistening red sores covering the whole of their diseased bodies. The scene might have been too much to handle for a man less accustomed to the horrors with which Ainsley Blake's sad and drawn-out existence had long since familiarised him. It seemed that the whole of the town had been bathed in blood and the shimmering red liquid, dancing in the light of a thousand surrounding fires, flowed through the streets, eventually drying into scarlet cement as it neared the fortifying heat given off by the flaming piles of dead. There, in that village of the damned, Blake was free to conduct himself in the manner which was the only means he believed could sustain his own life, and, although he did so with total impunity regarding potential legal ramifications, his conscience was not clear. He knew that he was not in any legal danger because, in a village comprised wholly of the sick and dying, death is not a question but a statement, and therefore no one is needed to answer for it. To die where death lives is to be expected, and suspicion does not exist because the hope for eventual justice that breeds it is absent in the hopeless.

Blake was not a bad man, however, and he reasoned that his actions were merciful. That to leave them to die by plague was infinitely crueller than to provide them the relief and dignity of a quick death. He searched among the horror for those he deemed to be enduring the greatest suffering and chose them first for his horrible purpose. He swore to himself that he took no pleasure in what he believed he had no choice in, but he had always known the unavoidable truth in his heart. The lion does not pity the gazelle, perhaps, but the lion is not human.

It was when Blake had left the wretched village and was returning to his own pristine estate that he came across her. At first, he saw nothing and rode in silence, torn, as he always was, by the unassuageable guilt of what had just transpired. In the silence, broken only by the regular hoofbeats of the loyal horse that he had unwittingly made party to something terrible, he heard a noise. It was a sort of groan, but weak and muddled, and seemed to emanate from a grove of trees offset from the main path. He stopped his horse and listened, terrified that his crimes had been witnessed, or worse, that the plague had breached the quarantine and crossed now onto his lands. A few minutes passed before he heard another groan, quieter than before. It seemed to him that whoever was there was growing weaker, and quickly. He stepped down from his horse and, patting her on the snout with both affection and authority, walked towards the source of the noise with careful steps.

As he approached more closely, he called out, "Hello there. Are you well? Do you need help?"

The groaning from within the grove continued, but there was no other answer. Blake resumed his approach until he perceived a pair of feet, adorned in muddy shoes that he recognised as both feminine and as made from the highest quality materials, sticking out from a pile of brush that obscured a body to which Blake knew they must be attached. He paused, thinking to himself that the fate of the prone figure would have been far more certain had he encountered her prior to his visit to the plague village. However, now that his crime of necessity had already been committed, he could not justify to himself committing another out of convenience, or even out of possible self-preservation.

He resolved, therefore, to render aid to the unlucky traveller and, by doing so, alleviate some of his own guilt and perhaps even repay a small debt to God, whom he was sure he offended often. In service to this resolution, he walked directly, and with purpose, until he reached the source of the suffering and, when he arrived by the figure's side and looked down, he found himself surprised by what he discovered there. He did not know what he had been expecting, but it had certainly not been this. The person whom had been so carelessly discarded into the roadside grove turned out to be a young girl and, though she was covered with mud and bloodied from head to toe, Blake could tell that she possessed incredible beauty.

"How did you end up like this?" he asked her, bending down. "Come on, let's get you out of here and cleaned up."

With the effortlessness one might observe in a healthy adult picking up a paperweight, Blake hoisted up the semi-conscious figure, carried her gently to his obediently waiting horse and placed her over the saddle. As he walked beside them back towards his estate house, the girl began to stir. He could see now more clearly how delicate her dirt-covered face truly was, and he allowed himself a slight smile as the sun rose in the east and painted a thousand shades of blue, orange and yellow across the brightening sky. With each passing stride, the dawning sky further illuminated her beautiful features and, though her circumstance was undoubtedly brought about by some great tragedy, it was the first time Blake could remember having known peace for many years. It was a fleeting peace, true, perceptible only for the briefest of moments, but Blake relished it as if it would last forever.

By the time they reached the house, the young girl's stirrings had become more frequent. Blake, watching her closely and registering every movement of her body, hoped with all his heart that she would be able to make a full recovery from injuries of which he did not yet know the full extent. He unloaded her carefully, his infallible horse standing perfectly still so as not to interfere with his progress, and succeeded in getting her into the front entrance hall, where he rang for his valet.

When the valet entered, looking as though he had still been in bed, Blake yelled, "Wake the handmaids and tell them to draw a bath!"

The valet, snapping out of his drowsiness upon seeing the wounded girl, turned and exited the atrium at a brisk pace, returning minutes later with a pair of tired-looking young women still in their dressing gowns.

Seeing Blake's incredulous look at having disobeyed a direct order, the valet responded quickly. "You will need help to carry her, sir, and the women will need to undress her and tend to her wounds."

Blake, conceding his valet's point, left the slowly waking girl in the care of the two handmaids before dropping into a plush chair by the front entrance in order to revisit the curious circumstances under which he had first come across her in the woods.

The valet, sensing that Blake's anger had receded far enough for him to safely venture a question, asked timidly, "Sir, if you don't mind me asking, what has happened this morning?"

Blake looked up at him, still thinking. "I do not mind, Colin. I was out for a morning ride and I came upon her lying in a grove just on the edge of the property. She was still alive but badly hurt, and so I brought her here. I know nothing else of her."

The valet gave Blake a concerned look and said, "Oh my. Sir, shall I wake the rest of the house?"

Blake looked up at him again, surprised, and was about to speak before the shrewd valet began again, sensing his master's vexation. "I am sorry, sir, that the house is not awake already, but it has been a very long time since you have required anything at all of us. You do not wish for us to prepare your meals and you keep only to a few rooms of the house and speak to no one. There simply is not much for us to do and so the house has taken to sleeping in most mornings."

Blake eyed the valet wearily and said, "You are quite right, Colin. I cannot expect you to be ready for an order that was unlikely ever to have been given. However, you must wake the house now and send a rider to town for a doctor straight away. Also, you will need to have a room made up for her until she is well. See that it's done with haste, Colin."

With this final order, the valet bowed deeply, proud to once again have a purpose in the noble house that he had spent his whole life serving, and exited to make the arrangements his master desired. Blake rose nervously and exited the entrance hall so that he could wait for a report as to the unknown young woman's condition just outside of the washroom in which the handmaids were tending to her.

What seemed to Blake like an eternity had passed when the door to the washing chamber finally opened and one of the handmaids, pink in the face and wearing a white apron stained with blood, emerged, searching her dress for a clean spot on which to dry her hands. Since she was looking down at her own soiled apron and not in front of her, she did not notice that Blake had been waiting just outside the door and nearly ran him over as she exited.

Spotting him just in time to avoid a collision, she gave a start and, panting with a hand over her heart, said, "Pardon me, sir. I did not know that you were there."

Blake, dispelling her apprehension with a wave of his hand that indicated the near-miss was far too low on his list of immediate priorities to be bothered with, said with some alarm, "What of the girl? Does she live?"

"She does, sir. Though she is very weak."

Blake put a hand to his chin in thought and then continued his interrogation, pacing back and forth in the hall. "She is awake then?"

The handmaid, still not fully recovered from the near-collision nor the abnormal events of the morning that had preceded it, answered timidly. "She is, sir, but she must rest now."

Blake breathed a sigh of relief and said, "Yes, of course. Colin has prepared a room for her. You can take her there for now. I have sent a rider for the doctor in town and I expect him here within the hour. I want someone to stay with her all the time until he arrives and informs us that it is safe to do otherwise."

The handmaid bowed her head in acknowledgement of her charge, and then turned to re-enter the wash chamber where the unknown guest and other handmaid were still engaged.

Before she disappeared into the room, she turned back to Blake one last time and said, "Sir, we will be bringing her through here. Perhaps it is best for now if you…"

Blake, recognising what it was she meant and taking the hint, answered, "Yes, of course. I will be in my study. If anything further is needed of me please do not hesitate. And come fetch me at once as soon as the doctor arrives."

The handmaid bowed her head once more and then disappeared into the other room, leaving Blake alone in the hall.

Another hour passed in high anxiety until a knock was heard on the study door, indicating that the doctor had arrived. Blake walked past the still-timid handmaid whom he had ordered to retrieve him, and straight to the entrance hall, where the doctor waited.

"Doctor. Thank you for coming with such haste. I am Ainsley Blake."

The doctor, a serious man who immediately made it clear that he had no intention of bothering with unnecessary pleasantries, said curtly, "That is very good. And where is the patient?"

Blake, knowing that time was a factor in the young woman's fate and so forgiving the doctor's rudeness, turned and said, "Follow me," as he walked quickly through the door at the far end of the hall with the stern doctor in tow behind him. When they reached the room that had been prepared for his unknown guest, Blake reached down for the doorknob.

Noticing this, the doctor quickly grabbed his hand and said, "Mr Blake, I think it will be best if I examine the patient alone. At least at first. If she is awake I will need to ask her a few questions regarding her condition and I will need her to be completely honest in her recollection. Having her rescuer, not to mention the master of this large estate, in the same room may disincline her to give me an honest account of what might have happened to her. It is best that she remains as at ease as it is possible for the time being."

Blake dropped his hand and said, "I understand. I will wait out here for you."

With a quick nod, the doctor turned the brass handle and entered the room, leaving Blake once again alone with his thoughts and fears.

As Blake waited outside of the bedroom for the doctor's return with the young girl's prognosis, he was unaware that his house, for many years a dark and sombre place, was suddenly teeming with life again. The household staff, feeling themselves to have a purpose once more, seemed to snap out of the morose lethargy that had plagued them ever since their young master had decided to disown the outside world, secluding himself within the dark corners of his large and empty house. Now, with the arrival of the injured young woman, the staff strolled about the house cleaning, lighting fires and smiling happily to one another as they passed in the halls. They had noticed a change in their sullen master the moment he had returned home with the mysterious girl.

Years prior to this, when his melancholy had still been new, his loyal and well-intentioned servants had often tried to engage their master in all manner of activities designed to induce an emotional response, trying desperately to pull him from the abyss that they feared would otherwise swallow him whole. Unfortunately, his apathy had outlasted their resolve, and, in the end, their discouragement was too great and so they too assumed their master's sorrow. Now, however, as if delivered from impassivity by the mere presence of the young girl, they saw genuine concern in his countenance, as well as pain and fear. The visage that had for years been a blank canvas, devoid of emotion, was now twisted with feeling, and they all knew that this meant something had changed. What it was or what it would mean, they did not know, but they knew that any change was welcome and they poured their souls back into the ancient home in order to accommodate it.

When the doctor finally emerged from the unlucky girl's bedroom, he found Blake precisely where he had said that he would be.

"Mr Blake," said the doctor seriously. "The girl will recover."

A flush of relief washed over Blake and he felt the tightness release that had been steadily building in his chest ever since arriving home. "Thank you, Doctor. I don't—"

"However," said the doctor, matter-of-factly, cutting Blake off. "She will need to stay here for the time being. She is far too weak to travel and she will need much rest."

Blake considered the proposition for a few moments and then said, "Of course, she is welcome for as long as she needs."

"Good," replied the doctor. "Now, I have done all I can for her today. She is awake if you need to speak with her, but she is still a bit confused and slightly afraid, so do not push her too hard. I will come back tomorrow morning to check on her."

Blake nodded in understanding, then asked, "But what happened to her, Doctor? I must know."

The doctor shook his head and answered, "I will let her tell you that only when, and if, she is ready. Good day, Mr Blake. I will see you first thing tomorrow."

After walking the doctor to the door and seeing him out, Blake returned to the hallway outside the unknown girl's room, torn as to whether or not he should disturb her. After a few minutes of fruitless internal deliberation, Blake recognised that he would enter the chamber regardless and so stopped trying to talk himself out of it. He further justified himself by concluding that it was much better to enter now, while the girl was almost certainly still awake, rather than pursue his contradicting line of thought to its inevitable conclusion and risk her falling back into unconsciousness, thus depriving him of the chance to speak with her until perhaps much later. Mastering his nerve, he raised a white-knuckled fist to the thick wooden door and knocked softly, not wanting to alarm her.

At first, Blake heard nothing from inside. Not a murmur, not a rustle. No indication of life whatsoever was perceptible from within the bedchamber.

Again summoning all of his available courage, which this second time seemed to cost him a great deal more than had the first, he knocked again and said, "Madam, I do not wish to disturb you, but I am Ainsley Blake. It was I who came across you on the road and brought you here to my family home."

He stopped to listen, leaning in so close that his ear nearly touched the dark wood of the door.

This time he heard slight stirrings from within and at last a quiet voice answered, "Please, come in."

At this invitation, Blake extended a shaking hand and grasped the brass knob, disengaging the latching mechanism that separated him from the girl.

A thousand thoughts coursed through Ainsley Blake's mind in the seconds that preceded his entry into the coveted bedchamber. The innumerable thoughts were so varied in their nature and so broad in their scope that, were they to occur in the mind of a normal man, it would take a lifetime to gain the experience necessary to process them, and an equal amount of time to have been able to produce them at all. Blake, however, followed each line of thought to its end in the mere seconds that elapsed as the door transitioned from closed to open.

Surprisingly, at the end of it all, the overall feeling was that of silliness. He was almost embarrassed, but not because the girl made him feel ill at ease. He was embarrassed to himself, privately. He knew that there was nothing on the Earth that could cause physical harm to him – at least not that he had ever encountered – and yet here he was with his hand shaking wildly at the prospect of meeting a young woman whom he had rescued from certain death only hours before. Undoubtedly, she would be greatly in his debt for the service he had rendered her, but still, his hand shook. It was not the first time that Blake had felt this way. It seemed that although his physical body was impervious to the infirmities that plagued his fellow man, his heart was anything but. He found that while his body had grown impermeable and strong, his capacity for feeling had remained very much as it always had been. Very much human.

It was due to this vulnerability, and human nature's unfortunate proclivity to exploit weakness, that had led to the tragic state of his family home. He had shut himself up, neglected his responsibilities, and left his staff without orders and in limbo. Now, standing outside of a bedchamber that belonged to him but sheltered another, and watching the door swing open on its hinges, he knew that his time shut away was over. He felt himself coming out into the light once more and his hand shook in anticipation of what that might mean. It shook in acknowledgement of the risk that he knew he was taking.

When the door finally opened to its full extent, revealing the flickering light within, Blake stepped into the chamber and quickly closed it again behind himself. In the bed, illuminated by the dancing light of the candles that surrounded her, was the girl. He had known that she was beautiful, even when her face had been obscured by blood and dirt, but now, clean-faced and timid, she looked to him as though she had been created by heaven for the sole purpose of becoming the new standard by which all future beauty would be measured. She gazed up at him with fear and hesitation in her shimmering eyes. Blake spoke softly, hoping to alleviate some of her obvious concern.

"Please, don't be afraid. You are very welcome here." He observed some of the tautness of her expression slacken and took this as a promising sign that he could proceed. "Allow me to reintroduce myself now that I am no longer on the other side of a large wooden door." Blake smiled at her softly, analysing her for any effect that his small joke may have produced, and continued, "I am Ainsley Blake and you are in my family's home."

Blake paused to give the girl some time to process this first piece of information. He was determined to take it slow and not overwhelm the poor girl during these crucial first moments that he hoped would mark the beginning of her convalescence.

When he was convinced that she had heard and understood what he had said, he continued, "I came across you while I was riding very early this morning."

He paused again, wondering if it was wise to give her all the details of the morning before she had had a chance to regain her strength. After a few moments of swift consideration, Blake decided that if the doctor had been comfortable in having her relive the tragic tale of how she had come to be on that roadside in the first place, then there must be no real danger in explaining to her how it was that he had come to find her there.

Satisfied with his reasoning, Blake went on. "I was riding along the eastern border of my land this morning when I heard a moaning just off the road. You could not be seen from the road, but I was able to follow the sound and it was not long before I found you in a grove of thick brush and vine. It looked as though you had been hidden there intentionally, left for dead, so that passers-by would be unable to locate you. Fortunately for you, it seems that death could not find you either and so I picked you up and brought you here straight away."

Blake finished his brief recount of the morning's events and then waited patiently for the young girl to speak.

After a few silent moments, the girl said quietly, "I owe you a great deal of gratitude, sir. A kindness like yours is rare in this world." Blake turned away, ashamed at receiving such a sincere compliment that he knew he did not deserve, but the girl continued, "I do not know what would have happened to me had you not come along. I suppose I would not have survived. Thank you, sir. I am in your debt eternally."

Blake turned back to face her and smiled. "You owe me nothing. My only wish is that you recover, and you must stay here until you regain your strength in full."

He wanted to ask her how it was that she had come to be lying on that roadside, but he sensed that she was not ready to tell him and so did not press her.

Instead he took her hand gently in his and kissed it softly, saying, "I will leave you to rest now. I have left a bell here on the table that you may ring if you are in need of anything. Colin, or one of the handmaids, will come if it is heard and they can bring you whatever you'd like. Sleep now and I will come again to check on you later this evening. The doctor will come again tomorrow morning."

Blake released her hand and turned to leave when the girl spoke once more, "Sir, do you wish to know my name?"

He nodded.

"It is Eugenia. Good day, sir."

And with this, Blake departed.

When he went to check on her later that evening, he found her sleeping peacefully and, taking that as a positive sign, decided to leave her undisturbed in order that she might sleep through the night.

Fortunately, it appeared that the rest had paid off when the following morning revealed a marked improvement in the girl's health. When Blake showed the doctor into her chamber, they found her out of bed and gazing through a bedroom window, very much as one might do following a particularly peaceful or reinvigorating night's sleep that hadn't been brought about by injury. To see her there, one could be forgiven for thinking that she was simply an invited guest of the great House of Blake, and that the circumstances that had brought her there were even festive in nature. It would be easy to imagine that the following evening would find her as the belle of some great ball designed to lift the once-great family out of obscurity and back into prominence.

The truth was that Eugenia, whose surname they learned to be Shepherd shortly after entering her chamber that morning, was very much recovered, at least compared to her precarious situation the previous night. The fact of the matter was that her wounds, though they had appeared grave at the time of their initial discovery, were far less critical than both the doctor and Blake had originally supposed. She had indeed suffered abrasions and bruising which had then been exacerbated by exhaustion and dehydration, but, on the whole, she was in no more physical danger than would be a small boy who, succumbing to the awkwardness of early age, falls to the ground and scrapes his knee, alarming his mother certainly, but in no real mortal peril.

When the two men entered, Eugenia greeted them with a smile so bright it seemed to intensify the rays of sunlight pouring in through the open window by a thousand times, catching both men off guard and leaving each with a feeling of unanticipated warmth. The effect was so powerful that the feelings of concern and seriousness with which the two men had entered were almost immediately supplanted with those of gratitude. Of the two struck men, the doctor was first to recover himself.

He beamed down at Eugenia with a smile of pure delight and said happily, "My dear, you are looking so well! How remarkable. How are you feeling? You must get back into bed, though. Please, I insist."

The doctor took her hand and led her back to the bed, ignoring her protestations and insisting that she needed to rest. Eugenia chatted merrily as the doctor examined her and when he had at last concluded that she was out of danger and began to pack up his bag, she thanked him profusely for his kindness. The atmosphere had become so jovial, in fact, that even the melancholy Blake could not resist participating, and he smiled and joined in the conversation cheerfully along with the rest.

This, of course, was not lost on the household staff, who listened outside the door and whispered amongst themselves as to the positive and unexpected change undergone by their master. The doctor lingered for a few minutes longer, apparently in no great hurry to separate himself from such a happy setting, but eventually excused himself, recognising mournfully that he had other appointments which, as a doctor, he had a moral obligation to keep. And, even though he was deservedly possessed with the pride of one who has conquered temptation in service to their principles, the doctor still regretted that these other appointments would undoubtedly be the sort to put a damper on his good mood. Eugenia thanked him once more and then Blake rose in order to walk him out.

As the doctor left, he turned back to the bright-eyed girl one last time and said, "It was truly a pleasure, Ms Shepherd. Should you ever need anything, please do not hesitate."

With this he gave her a quick nod, turned to Blake and shook his hand, and then departed, leaving the two young people alone together once more.

In the days that followed, the house seemed fit to burst at the seams with the new life that had been breathed into it with Eugenia's arrival. At Blake's insistence, and to the delight of the household at large, she had agreed to stay at the sprawling estate through the winter in order to fully regain her strength. In the first few days that followed the harrowing morning of her arrival, the interior of the house had been transformed from a dark, dusty and lifeless cavern into a fire-warmed, sunlit home, bustling with activity and laughter. The staff could not believe their good fortune and could often be found peering around corners or peeking out from behind partially closed window curtains in order to catch a glimpse of their master and his guest, hoping that this time spent together was blossoming into something deeper and more lasting. There was indeed a unanimous fear amongst the staff that if the girl were to leave, the reborn house would inevitably fall back into despair, perhaps even more deeply than before and, while they had weathered the first downfall of the great house and emerged now on the other side, they were not sure that they possessed the resilience to survive a second plummet.

Fortunately, for both Blake and his staff, the rescue of a human life always plants a seed of gratitude in the heart of the person rescued and, given time and proximity, that seed is easily cultivated into a binding love for the hero who has delivered one from death's icy grip. Without realising it in those first few weeks of her stay, Eugenia was in the preliminary grips of a powerful love that would bind her eternally to the one who had given back her life.

In the heart of Ainsley Blake, too, there had been planted a seed of gratitude, though different in its form. There was certainly no one in this world who could give him what he had an unlimited supply of already, that is to say the form of life he had given to Eugenia that meant a beating heart and working lungs. Moreover, he would have infinitely more gratitude for the person who was able to destroy it rather than preserve it. However, there was something which she had given him all the same and it was that which was now sacred to him. It was not life, as life is commonly defined, but instead the courage and desire to live it. The reclusive Blake emerged from his hiding and the people of the surrounding lands celebrated the return of their long-absent lord. Everything that Eugenia touched seemed instantly transformed from gloomy to sparkling, and everyone at whom she smiled seemed inspired to achieve greatness in whatever task they had at hand.

After a few months of playfulness and tiptoeing around what was already obvious to the entire household, the pair openly declared their love to one another and announced plans to marry just as soon as the snow melted. This announcement was met with thunderous applause from the whole of the born-again household.

When the snow finally did melt a week later, Eugenia declared that she needed to ride for her family home straight away in order to deliver the news – not only of her marriage, but also of her own well-being. It seemed hard to believe that she had been absent and unable to send word for many months due to the severity of the weather, and she knew that her family was likely sick with worry. Perhaps they were even on the verge of giving up hope altogether, or maybe they already had. Her family, after all, had been expecting her home many months ago when tragedy had unexpectedly befallen her. She decided that as soon as the emotion that would undoubtedly accompany her return home had tapered off, she would announce her intentions to marry her rescuer, that peculiar master of the noble house of Blake.

Blake himself, uncomfortable at the prospect of letting her ride off again but compelling himself to be understanding of her need to go without him, sent several armed escorts along with her in order to ensure that she did not meet with a similar fate as she had on her previous excursion.

With the arrangements made, Eugenia kissed her fiancé softly on the cheek and said, "I will return to you in two weeks' time with my father's blessing. Until then I will have nothing in my heart but you."

Blake released her hands and helped her onto the finest horse from his stables. He stood with the entire staff of the household at his back, watching her leave. They had all gathered to bid their safe travels to the one who had delivered them from idleness and sorrow, and, as she rode away into the distance, they all prayed for her swift return. After a few moments, the servants returned to their tasks and only Blake remained, still watching, until he could no longer perceive the black dot of the riding party on the horizon. When he was sure that she had really gone, he turned and re-entered the house alone.

Two weeks later, Blake sat in a chamber with thick stone walls, staring into the fire and wondering impatiently when his beloved might return. She had sent word a few days previously that she would be arriving today and, in his excitement, he found himself constantly glancing at the chamber entrance, expecting it to fly open at any minute and reveal the one whom he loved.

Realising his own silliness in constantly monitoring the entry door, however, he attempted to distract himself by studying the banners on the wall. His gaze ran over the various insignia until it fell upon a handsome crest that bore a red square, shot through on all sides by thick red bars, with the name "Blake" inscribed beneath it in a well-practised hand. The family crest.

After a few moments spent musing over his own responsibilities as the current head of Blake house, his thoughts turned to his father, the first Ainsley Blake, from whom he had taken his name. There was a secret that had long oppressed the current Blake. He had gone to great lengths to keep this secret safe and now that the first Ainsley Blake no longer lived, he was the only living soul that retained any knowledge of it. He feared what would become of him if it was ever discovered that this first Ainsley Blake was not, in actuality, his father at all.

Many years prior to the current Lord Blake's betrothal, when the elder Blake still lived and the house was at its peak of greatness, the great forerunner found himself visiting a province that fell under the jurisdiction of his great house and had recently been decimated by some unknown evil. As the elder Blake rode amongst the ruins, searching for survivors, he felt his hope quickly begin to slip away in the face of the unimaginable devastation. He dispatched experts in all fields to unearth the root cause of the province's destruction and the mass dying of its people, but no culprit would ever be identified in the time that followed. The heartbroken elder Blake was just about to call off his search for survivors when he perceived movement within the smouldering remains of a small cabin.

Dismounting his great steed, he approached the source of the movement, calling out, "Is there anyone alive in there? If so, then by God, speak!"

After a few moments of silence, a figure rose solemnly from the ashes. It was a young man, soot covered and in rags, his face torn by grief.

The elder Blake gasped, "My God! Come here, my son!"

The young man approached timidly and the elder Blake kindly covered him with his own long travelling cloak.

"You must be freezing! Take this and tell me what has happened here?"

The young man did not speak and the old man did not push him.

"Well, you come with me now. We will get you fed and cleaned up. You must be starving."

The young man allowed himself to be led away and, riding directly behind the elder Blake on the back of his great steed, found himself a few hours later at the gates of the vast Blake estate.

In the weeks that followed, the elder Blake would never receive a full account as to what exactly had occurred in that cursed province in which he had found the young man. In the end, he attributed the lone survivor's silence on the matter to the trauma of having survived such a horrific event and, determined not to make the young man relive it, contented himself with never knowing its cause. The mystery, however, was further intensified when it was discovered that the young man was completely devoid of any name, or at least any name that he was willing to share. In the end, the old man had settled on calling him simply: "Son".

Though the young man fully regained his health almost immediately upon arriving at the estate, he was invited to stay on at the Blake house indefinitely. He was able to find employment on the grounds and the old man, delighted at acquiring such a fine young protégé, formally educated him, dined with him each night and even gave him one of the home's finest rooms for use as his private chambers. The elder Blake, never married and without an heir, took the young man he had rescued under his wing and treated him as the son that he had never been able to sire himself.

After several happy years spent in this fashion, the adoption was made legitimate in the eyes of the law and the name of Ainsley Blake was officially bestowed upon the now well-manicured and charming young man. In addition, he was declared the sole heir of Blake house and successor to the lordship. Many more years later, as the old man lay dying on his bed, he made his adopted son swear to always uphold the honour of the house. The new Lord Blake agreed without hesitation and held his father's hand tenderly as the beloved patriarch and mentor entered death's final throes, and then was no more. The young Blake emerged from the death chamber, weighed down with a sorrow that would plague him for many years to come, as the new lord and master of the ancient house.

Blake turned his gaze from the family crest on the wall and realised with shame that he had not fulfilled the promise he had made to the man who had become his father. It was true that the nobility of the house was still intact and untarnished by scandal, but it had undoubtedly fallen in esteem from the lofty heights of its former glory. It was also true that now, so many years after the elder Blake's death, not a soul remained living who could have borne witness to the current Blake's origin, nor his subsequent adoption into the household.

His secret was safe. Death had hidden it forever within the tombs of those who had served his father, but his unfulfilled promise still tormented him. He glanced again at the wooden door, but there was still no sign of Eugenia's return. He was beginning to grow worried but consoled himself with the knowledge that long-distance travel was rarely a thing that could be predicted with any certainty. He knew in his heart that Eugenia was the key to the return to glory of his father's house. That what the provinces needed was a new lady whom they could love and serve. Her brightness was not reserved for Blake alone – that he knew and would not be so selfish as to demand it. Her grace would spread throughout the land like a sunrise and bring light and happiness to everything it touched, as it had done already for his wretched house and those who dwelled within it.

When the door finally flew open, it was not Eugenia but Colin who entered, looking highly distressed.

"Sir, you must come with me. Quickly!"

Blake rose from his seat and flew to his valet with inhuman speed. Grabbing his shoulders, he said with urgency, "What is it, Colin? Is it Eugenia?"

"I know not, sir! Please come!"

Colin ran from the room with Blake following closely at his heels. They emerged from the front entrance of the house into a crowd comprised of all the other household staff who had already congregated on the front lawn, all looking with interest at something off on the horizon. Blake followed their gaze into the darkness and saw immediately what it was that had aroused their curiosity and alarm.

Far in the distance, but steadily growing larger, were what looked like hundreds of disembodied, dancing flames, flickering and bouncing from side to side. What the flames connected to remained obscured by darkness, but Blake knew with certainty that the flames belonged to torches, and that the carriers of those torches were not likely to be on a mission of peace. The innumerable shining orbs were so vast that they looked like stars painted against the blackness of the horizon, extending the reach of heaven deep into the realm of man so that the division between the two spheres could no longer be perceived. Blake knew that the torch-bearing men likely believed themselves to be doing the work of God and smiled cynically, recognising the irony and preparing himself to meet them in peace, if possible. Colin, seeing the advancing torches, gasped in fear and retreated back into the house. The other staff, more desirous of witnessing something novel and potentially tragic than of ensuring their own safety, remained rooted to the spot at the back of their master.

When the silhouettes of those bearing the torches finally gained a true form through the darkness, Blake called out, "Who goes there? You are trespassing on my lands and I demand an explanation. This is not the conduct of civilised men to storm the house of a noble with undeclared intentions in the dead of night."

It was a round-bellied man of average height and about thirty years of age who answered him. "Hold your tongue, Lord Blake. We are making the demands tonight, sir."

Blake, fixing the man with a calculating stare that was full of venom, replied, "You are aware that I could have you hanged for this?"

The man did not answer but turned to one of his subordinates in the crowd behind him and said, "Bring him forward."

There was a murmuring in the crowd, followed by a shuffling, and then someone emerged from the interior at the round man's side. This new man was gaunt and pockmarked, and he walked with such a pronounced limp that Blake was certain that he would collapse with each stride. He did not hold a torch, and when Blake followed his thin arms down to his hands to see why, he noticed that they were each frozen tight in unmovable fists and blackened with the tell-tale signs of advanced gangrene. This man was not able to hold a torch – he was not able to hold anything at all.

The round man spoke again. "Tell him what you saw, Turner."

Being called forth like this in the face of the great Lord Blake, and then asked to recount the reason for which they had come, seemed to be too much for the invalid, and he said nothing for a few moments. Instead, he stared petrified at Blake's narrowed eyes, seemingly unable to move.

The round man put a consoling arm on the frightened man's shoulder and said in a reassuring tone, "Go on, Turner. No one can hurt you here. Tell us all what you saw."

Turner, seemingly emboldened by this consolation, pointed a single, mummified fist straight at Blake and said, "Him! I saw him! It was he who decimated my village."

The sickly man paused as Blake's staff absorbed the accusation with gasps and mutterings, then went on. "He came in the night, destroying the sick, dying and healthy alike. I watched as he moved from soul to soul, leaving each as a corpse behind him. He left only the dead untouched and it was that for which he mistook me. Only I was not dead, only dying. I lay in the mud, paralysed by my disease and by fear, and watched powerlessly as all the life was drained from our village. When he departed, it was only I who remained breathing. And though I thought death was certain, it never came for me. Instead, my condition gradually improved, and eventually I was found and cared for. Now, though I am disfigured, and my feet and hands rot and fall from my body in clumps of black flesh, I can still serve righteousness by revealing our own Lord Blake for what he truly is. A demon!"

A roar of anger and condemnation surged from the torch-bearing crowd in the wake of the stricken Turner's words. Blake, however, appeared to remain perfectly calm.

He scanned the crowd mildly and then answered the accusation simply. "My dear Mr Turner. You have undoubtedly suffered immensely, and you have my deepest sympathy and most sincere condolences. However, what you say you witnessed was not reality, for how could it be? You were stricken and in the grips of a madness brought on by fever. By the grace of God, you seem to have persevered, and we are all thankful for that, but the horrors you have had to endure seem to have left their mark upon you. It is not uncommon for those at the mercy of a great fever of the brain to perceive that which is not so, and you should therefore carry no shame for the baseless accusations which you have brought forth here today. You have my condolences and my forgiveness. I will see to it personally that you are taken care of in your convalescence."

Blake gestured to one of the servants still gathered at his back and he entered the house, returning moments later with a small pouch that bulged with something that was jingling with each step. When the bag was placed into Blake's hand, and it looked as though he was going to speak again, the round-bellied man spoke first.

"So, you deny the accusations then?" He looked around at the others in his mob as if for encouragement, and then continued, "We happen to have a witness from within your own house, sir."

This new piece of information, much to the delight of his accuser, appeared to bring forth a slight alteration in Blake's countenance. The change was so tiny and fleeting that it was nearly impossible to perceive, but the round man had recognised in it all that he had needed to assure his case.

Relishing this small but significant shift in the manner of the accused and determining not to squander his chance now that his intended victim appeared to have let go some ground, the mob leader signalled directly to two of his larger accomplices. Obeying their appointed leader, the two hulking men immediately came forth, breaking through the crowd of Blake's staff and entering the manor house without bothering to ask permission. Shuffling and banging sounds from within indicated that the two intruders were not making any attempt to be respectful of the house's many great and priceless artefacts. When the two large men finally emerged, they were dragging a kicking and screaming Colin between them, his expression contorted with shame and fear. They threw the pitiful man at Blake's feet, where he immediately began howling with regret.

"Please forgive me, sir! Please! They threatened to kill me if I did not tell them the truth of where it is you go at night! Please, sir, I could not bear it! Have mercy!"

Blake looked down at the servant whom he had trusted above all others, and who now had betrayed him, and felt both rage and pity at once, but acted on neither.

Instead, he turned his gaze back to the round-bellied leader of the mob and said calmly, "What is your intention then, sir?"

The man, somewhat unnerved by Blake's calmness, answered, "You shall come with us peacefully and you will face charges. You are under arrest. And, just so you do not get any ideas…"

The man yet again signalled behind him and the crowd shifted in response once more. This time what emerged shook Blake to his core. It was Eugenia, bound and bleeding, red blood glistening fresh down the front of her white dress. Blake took a step forward and the whole mob let out a collective gasp.

"Don't try anything foolish, Lord Blake," said the round man in alarm. "The girl will be spared if you simply comply."

Blake stopped, recognising the hopelessness of his situation and dropping his head in defeat, saying, "Yes, of course I will not resist."

Despite Blake's apparent submission, it seemed that his initial advance towards the mob had incited a spark of panic from somewhere within the mass of torch-lit people. That spark, fanned by proximity, superstition and darkness, grew almost immediately into a full-fledged flame of hysteria that spread like wildfire throughout the crowd.

People began to grow restless and started shouting, "Destroy him! He must be destroyed now!" and, "We cannot risk arresting him! This must end tonight!"

The round-bellied man desperately attempted to reassure the surging mob but to little effect. Once the initial spark had been pushed beyond its originator, its progression became exponential throughout the congregation, inciting a chain reaction that was quickly beyond all hope of stopping. The former leader found his authority wholly and instantaneously subverted by the collective hysteria of a mob that he had himself assembled.

Blake, recognising the danger present in the deteriorating calm of the crowd, and having thoughts only for Eugenia's safety, advanced again, more slowly this time, with his hands raised high to avoid further inciting the rage of the crowd, and even with a fleeting hope of potentially being of assistance in restoring calm.

His advance had the opposite effect, however, and the crowd became even more disjointed and violent. Blows started flying amongst its members as those in the middle attempted to flee but found themselves blocked in by their comrades on all sides. The faces, at first yellow by firelight, now glowed red with blood as the fight erupted, engulfing the entire group in chaos and confusion. It was clear that the original cause of the panic was already forgotten, but they fought anyway, unsure exactly as to why or to what end. They had come to slay a demon, but instead fought each other. Blake watched Eugenia in terror as she was pulled back and forth by the ends of the ropes that bound her.

Dust rose up from underneath a hundred pairs of shuffling, trampling feet, obscuring the entire scene so that Blake could no longer see or liberate his love. Voices rose to a scream and confusion overtook any reason that remained to them. It was only when the fateful blade, wielded by an unknown hand, descended across Eugenia's left shoulder and she fell, lifeless, to the ground, that all movement suddenly stopped.

As death overcame her, the hysteria that had fractured the mob seemed to die instantly alongside her. Chaos was supplanted by shock, horror and silence. The quiet persisted unbroken for many long moments. It was the heavy, unfathomable silence that always follows in the wake of a great tragedy, especially when that tragedy was brought about unnecessarily by the weaknesses of human nature. When one suddenly and unwittingly finds one's self as party to some great moral infraction that they had not intended to commit. The death of an innocent seemed to restore reason to the panting crowd, but it was too late to save her. They all knew that in the eyes of Lord Blake, the sin had been committed and repentance would not bring salvation.

As the dust settled, Blake stared down at his beloved. A dark red pool spread in a circle from beneath her, turning the surrounding dirt to clay. For a long time no one spoke. No one moved. Everyone stared at Blake, wondering what might happen next. After what seemed like an eternity, a few of those whose torches had not gone dark in the fray noticed the nobleman's hands ball into fists, and his head raise slowly to face the crowd. There was no humanity in his hollow, black eyes. No sadness, nor civility. His face was primal, animalistic and snarling, as is the face of a lioness whose cubs have been threatened. His face was that of a predator that has been cornered and has no recourse but violence in its most pure form. Not for honour, not for glory, not for gain of any kind. Violence for the sake of pain. Violence for vengeance.

No survivor of that night would later be able to relate what exactly had transpired next. In the weeks that followed, the massacre would remain as shrouded in mystery as it had been on the night it had occurred. Blake seemed to vanish right before their eyes. The next thing they knew, dirt was rising in a vortex, sealing in the mob on all sides, and all of the air seemed to be sucked from the atmosphere. Everyone dropped to their knees, gasping for breath and clawing at their throats, unable to see anything or breathe. The dirt pelted their skin like tiny knives, and their eyes watered.

Suddenly, at the moment they believed they would lose consciousness, air returned to them. The dust vortex stopped spinning and the airborne particles began to settle once more. The survivors took enormous, life-giving gulps of dusty air, coughing and sputtering. Some vomited up dirt clods, stained red from their damaged lungs, and some bled from the eyes and ears. When the air finally cleared completely, there remained only an unmoving pile of the guilty dead. Among them were all the members of the invading mob and, on the very top of the pile, lay Colin, unforgiven and shamed, even in death.

Among the survivors were the remaining household staff, innocent in this tragedy and therefore spared by their master. Missing from amongst both the dead and the living were Blake himself and the body of his murdered beloved.

A loud crash from behind them caused the staff to turn sharply away from the unholy pile. Flames leaped from the windows of the handsome Blake house and moments later, the entire estate was consumed in red fire. The survivors stood in silence, holding each other in solidarity, as they watched the home they had spent their entire lives serving reduced to ashes. They wept on each other's shoulders. The wept for what they had been through, for what they had seen, and they knew that they would carry the horror of that night with them for the rest of their lives.

They wept for the master that they had loved, and that they knew was gone now forever. They wept for the innocent girl whom he would never marry, and the injustice which she had suffered. They wept for the noble house of Blake, a pillar of honour and dignity for so many generations, gone now, forever, in a night.

-XII-

A INSLEY BLAKE SNAPPED BACK FROM HIS PAINFUL recollections, returning to the comfortable library of his handsome Georgian manor house. He was still staring out the window and into the darkness of a sky that looked eerily similar to that which had presided over the terrible events of that fateful night. As he considered this, a meteor suddenly shot across the sparkling horizon, followed closely by its luminous silver tail, imparting finally some point of distinction upon this sky of the present day. A single star among billions, rebelling against its own place in the heavens and, for a brief moment of unimpeachable glory, shining brighter than any of its fellows.

Blake followed the fiery ball with his eyes until it reached its sputtering end and then shook his head, trying to empty it of the painful memories that he had revisited tonight for the first time in many years. He wondered what had called them forth after so long. Perhaps it was the night sky, so like that under which tragedy had befallen him so long ago. Perhaps it was the name Ainsley Blake, which he had abandoned that same night out of necessity.

Following the downfall of his father's house, Blake had been forced to assume a variety of subsequent identities. At first, it was simply to avoid being hunted down by the sovereigns of England, but eventually he was forced to do this in order to avoid dangerous questions regarding his own longevity, which he knew he would be unable to answer in a manner suitable in the eyes of the church.

It had only been in preparation for his most recent voyage to the New World that Blake had decided to reassume the moniker that had meant so much more to him than had any other throughout the course of his long existence. He'd had the romantic idea that by once again taking on the name of his beloved and adopted father, he might perhaps gain yet another opportunity to fulfil the promise he had made to the dying man so many years ago, which still haunted him to this day.

Though these reasons were compelling in their own right, Blake knew that neither the night sky nor his great name were the instruments by which the painful memories of his past had been called forth at long last. It was Ginny. It was she who had awoken his heart, and she who carried with her the strength of his murdered love that had so moved him when he had first perceived it in her. The feelings that she inspired in him were the same as those that had doomed her predecessor. The love of Ainsley Blake was not a gift, but a sentence, passed by an unseen judge and destined to go un-lifted throughout eternity. Blake feared for what it meant. He knew that if history were to repeat itself, he would be unable to bear it. His heart could not abide another Eugenia.

A few weeks later Ginny sat hand in hand with Blake at one of their favourite tables at Proust, nervously awaiting her father's arrival. Today was the day on which he was to finally meet the man who had stolen his daughter's heart and she was accordingly nervous at the prospect. She had been anxious to make the introduction ever since the water enclosure debate during which she had, in consequence of her father's interrogation, confessed the truth regarding the sudden decline in her availability. Ginny had perceived a hint of alarm and disapproval in her father's reaction that day and, though he covered those reactions deftly and quickly, she who knew him best had noticed them. For a while, she had allowed herself to be falsely lulled into contentment, hoping naively that she had been mistaken, but she now desired for him to see the man as he appeared to her as soon as possible, so as to put him, and perhaps herself even more so, at ease. The fact that several weeks had needed to elapse before she was able to secure the meeting between the two most important men in her life had been a source of constant vexation for her. Even Dub had perceived her irascibility down at the marina and found himself walking on eggshells whenever he was near her.

Her stress had come on so abruptly in the wake of the fleeting happiness that her father's false assurances had given her that, on the evening following the great reveal, Ginny found herself sleepless, lying in her bed and staring up at the ceiling. It took many hours before exhaustion had finally overtaken her anxiety and she fell into a restless slumber. Her apprehension, however, did not relent with sleep and she found herself suddenly in the grips of a terrible nightmare.

She dreamed that she had been torn from the arms of her lover and then made to parade in front of him as a means of torture. The crowd that held her back pulsed with rage, hatred and fear, all directed at him, and she did not understand why. The next thing she knew, a great barrier had risen and blinded her, cutting her off from him. Though she felt no pain, she knew that the crazed people on either side of her were tearing her limb from limb and that the chaos of the stampede was preventing her rescue at the hands of her great love.

When something cold and shining like fire descended upon her and she was sure that she would die, she awoke, dripping with sweat. The nightmare seemed as authentic as anything that had ever happened to her, and she had remained very still for a long time in her bed, shaking and holding her knees to her chest. Eventually she rose from the bed, giving up on sleep for the night, and sat herself in the sill of her large bedroom window to look at the stars. They seemed, as they always did, to restore to her some semblance of peace and, when she saw the beautiful, fiery orb cut a bright path across the night sky, she marvelled at its majesty.

When the old man entered Proust, looking as young as ever, Blake and Ginny both rose to greet him.

"Hi, Daddy!" squealed Ginny as she ran up to him and threw her arms around his neck.

"Hello, sweetheart," replied the old man, keeping both of his eyes trained on Blake.

When they parted, Ginny turned excitedly to Blake and, indicating him with both hands as if he was a meal and her father some hungry consumer, said excitedly, "Dad, this is Ainsley Blake. Ainsley Blake, this is my dad."

The old man, with considerable effort, smiled brightly at his daughter and then turned to Blake, extending his hand.

Blake, seeing the smile and taking note of what it was costing the old man to maintain the farce in front of his daughter, took the outstretched hand and said, "It's a pleasure to meet you, sir. Ginny has told me a great deal about you. I'm just sorry it has taken this long."

"Not at all," said Ginny's father. "It's very nice to meet you as well. Ginny tells me that you are from London?"

"Yes, sir, that is correct," answered Blake. "I lived there until recently when I decided that I preferred a quieter life."

"Well, you've certainly found it here," replied the old man.

The trio took their seats at the table and spoke on in generalities like this for the next hour or so. Ginny did most of the talking, mainly pointing out Blake's many fine attributes, and shot her father periodic glances in an attempt to read his expression. To her delight, her father looked genuinely pleased and when she had contented herself that she had read the old man's face accurately, she turned her gaze to Blake in order to obtain a similar reading.

She noticed that he too seemed to be enjoying himself and beamed at both of them as they spoke on.

What Ginny was not able to perceive at the table was that, in reality, much more information than she could have ever dreamed of was passing between her father and Blake. She saw two happy men, both of whom meant the world to her, engaged in a cheerful conversation of no greater depth than could be expected from surface-level pleasantries about people, places and things. The two men, however, both adept in concealing their true feelings in the face of those whom they wished to remain in the dark, understood that there was something far deeper between them that needed to be addressed. When Ginny rose from the table and announced that she needed to use the lady's room, the old man seized the opportunity.

"We need to speak. Privately. Away from my daughter."

Blake considered him for a moment and then answered, "Yes. We can speak alone while Ginny is at the marina tomorrow. We will need someplace private."

"Come to my house at 10am tomorrow morning…" the old man said, jotting something down on his napkin and handing it to Blake. "…here is the address. The house will be empty. Don't be late."

Blake pocketed the napkin just as Ginny reappeared, smiling, at the table.

"There was a line at the bathroom. No worries, I can hold it. So, what were you guys talking about?"

Both men looked up at her and smiled, stood in politeness so that she could retake her seat and then sat back down themselves in order to reassume their charade.

The next morning, a full fifteen minutes before the clock hit ten, Ainsley Blake waited outside the superbly kept house of Ginny's father. He was determined not to be late and so had left his own house with plenty of time, but now that he was here with time to spare, he found that he did not want to be early either. After a few more minutes spent watching the superfluous happenings of the neighbourhood, Blake's need to face the old man finally won out over his determination not to be early. Shrugging and abandoning his punctuality as a futile attempt, he headed towards the front door with still a full ten minutes to spare. He arrived at the large wooden door and reached for the bronze knocker but, before he had even made contact with it, the large door swung open of its own accord, revealing the old man.

"Mr Harrison," said Blake with a quick nod.

"Come in, Blake," answered the old man without emotion. "As I suspect that you are not a man with whom I need to exchange pleasantries before making my point known, please allow me to get right to it." The old man, turning to face Blake now that the front door had closed behind them, said seriously, "I know what you are."

Blake, showing no reaction at all, replied simply, "Undoubtedly you do."

The old man glared at him and Blake met his gaze. Both men sized each other up, scanning for weaknesses.

It was Blake who continued, "I had not perceived it the night I first saw you outside the theatre. To be sure, I was so taken with your daughter's beauty that I did not have eyes for much else." Blake began to pace as he spoke. "When you walked into the coffee shop today, however, I sensed it immediately." Blake stopped pacing and turned again to face the old man. "You, too, are like me. Does Ginny know?"

The old man, taking his turn now to not be surprised, spoke simply, "No. She does not. And she mustn't ever find out."

The old man's head dropped in shame, stricken now with worry, but he continued, "I have worked too hard to protect her. You know as well as I do the risks inherent when we allow ourselves to love. I am not wrong in supposing you to have, in your past, lost many of those closest to you simply because of what you are?"

Blake nodded in acknowledgment that he had. A thousand thoughts ran through his mind. Not long ago, he had believed himself to be the only one, and now in this small Georgian town, he had twice already encountered others. He did not know how to process the information. On one hand, he was glad, having been alone and hopeless for so long. On the other, he feared that this man would attempt to tear him from Ginny. He did not know what to do and he needed time to think. To his surprise, however, when the old man spoke again, his words were not the demand for a separation from his daughter that Blake had been expecting.

"I know that I cannot force you to part from my daughter, Mr Blake. And, seeing the way you look at her, I know that you cannot compel yourself to part from her either. People like us have lived long enough to have borne witness to countless loves, and only we can truly understand that when consumed by it, there is no peril so great as to prevent us from seeking it. No, I cannot stop you. You are stronger, true, but I would not venture to try even if that were not so."

Blake stared at the old man as he spoke, astonished.

The old man continued in a sadder tone, "I only ask, Blake, that you protect her. That you do everything in your power to keep her safe and your true nature hidden from her." The old man grabbed Blake's hands, pleadingly, and went on more loudly. "Promise me, Blake! A woman in love will not listen to her father, but a man of reason might listen to the father of the woman he loves when he knows that what he says is true."

The old man released Blake's hands without waiting for his promise and walked over to a small table against a far wall. He picked up what looked like newspaper clippings and then went on, again approaching Blake. "I have seen this business of the realtor, Obadiah Davids, and the old man, Lange, and this is what must stop. They were studied choices, true, but still obvious to me and, therefore, potentially others as well."

He tossed the newspaper scraps on the ground and again seized Blake's hands. "Swear to me, Blake. Swear that you will not endanger my daughter."

Blake, totally taken aback and unable to find words at first, stammered something nonsensical. The old man held his gaze, waiting for Blake's promise.

Blake cleared his throat and said, this time with more composure, "I will not bring any danger to her. The times are different today than what we have experienced in the past. Man is cynical and disbelieving now. He will believe only what is comfortable to believe. He will believe whatever gives him peace for he clings to it desperately. Life is lived out of convenience today and the abnormal is buried so that the normal does not have to be reminded of its existence. I will keep her safe, and so will you. You do not stop being a father to a daughter simply because she has learned to invite another man into the part of her heart that a father cannot occupy. She will need you now more than ever, and you will need her as you always have."

The old man released Blake's hands and looked slightly relieved. What Blake said made a lot of sense to him and the feeling of impending doom that he had carried with him since the day his daughter had announced her courtship began to seem like it might be an outdated line of thought. The two men stood looking at each other for a long while without saying anything.

Finally, drawing a deep breath and exhaling slowly, the old man said, "Thank you, Blake," and walked the man his daughter loved to the front door.

-PART THREE-

- I -

B RUCE KELLY SQUINTED INTO THE SUNLIGHT AS HE GLANCED down the town's desolate main street. He had never been to Georgia before and he found that he didn't care for it much now that he was here. Gathering the phlegm from deep in the back of his throat, he hocked a thick loogie grumpily into the street and then turned back to the sidewalk. He walked a few more blocks and then, realising that he didn't have anything better to do, turned into a coffee shop with some stupid French-sounding name that he wasn't due to arrive at for another fifteen minutes.

Bruce was forty-two years old and originally from Johannesburg, South Africa. He'd started getting into trouble when he was a kid and had been unable to keep himself out of it ever since. Attending a school growing up that had largely consisted of British-descended whites had taught him at a young age how to hate his fellow man.

The focal point of his hate at that time, engendered in him by the political atmosphere in which he was raised, had been the Afrikaner people, or Dutch-descended whites. He hadn't really known why he hated them, only that he was supposed to because his great-grandfather had died fighting them in the Second Boer

War. He would have hated Africa's native people as well, had he bothered to consider them as people at all. He viewed them, as did all African whites, simply as a nuisance, a type of pest, and, growing up in the grips of apartheid, there were very few authority figures that harboured any inclination to tell him otherwise.

One day, after a particularly brutal fight during which a thirteen-year-old Bruce had hospitalised one of the boys that lived down the street, his parents had finally seen fit to remove him from the negative influence of the friends with whom he ran and who were, in their opinion, the cause of his bad behaviour. Thinking also that another big city might lead to similar problems, his parents had decided to move the whole family to a small ranch in Botswana, where they had remained until Bruce came of age.

When Bruce turned eighteen, he left home forever and took the first job he was offered as an assistant and protégé to a professional hunter who worked on a big game ranch bordering the celebrated Okavango Delta. He quickly proved himself to be a fast learner and surprised everyone at the ranch with the prodigious skill he showed in wielding a rifle.

Not surprisingly, being naturally gifted in the deadly art of shooting advanced him quickly in his rank and within the first few months of his employment at the ranch, he found himself out in the field with the hunting groups rather than chained to an administration desk with the other new hires.

It was on his third or fourth expedition that he first encountered poachers. His party had come across them when vultures circling overhead had alerted them to the possibility that some large game might be lying dead just outside the tree line, usually an indication of trouble and always worth looking into, since vultures only feed on what is freshly dead. They followed the radial line provided to them by the scavenging birds to the centre of their flight path where, as they had feared, a large, unmoving mass lay still. Approaching more closely revealed that the mass was an extremely rare rhinoceros, shot countless times and mutilated solely for the value its horn possessed in certain uninformed Asian markets.

Bruce had certainly been aware prior to this that poachers were rampant out on the savannah, and that a rhino horn was amongst the most coveted of all the potential bounty harvested from the animals that were targeted, but he had never experienced it first-hand and wasn't sure exactly how to react now that he had. He found that he did not share in the feelings of horror and disgust present in the party's other members. In fact, he found, to the contrary, that he was not moved at all. Sure, he was missing out on a little cash by not being able to sell the right to shoot this animal to some Western tourist, but he didn't feel any compassion or sympathy for the animal itself, though it had been destroyed without reason or mercy.

As Bruce looked down, examining the dead rhinoceros on the ground, he heard someone yell, "Look! The tracks are still fresh!"

As if this announcement had initiated some sort of protocol of which Bruce had been heretofore unaware, all the members of the hunting party climbed into their Land Rovers and, calling to Bruce to hop in, sped off in the direction of the tracks. They didn't have to drive far before they found who they were looking for. As their vehicles burst from the tree line into a clearing they saw at the other end a group that clearly wasn't supposed to be there. Bruce's boss, who was riding next to him in the same vehicle, yelled for the other vehicles to remain in pursuit while ordering his own driver, much to Bruce's surprise, to keep them stopped where they were.

Pulling a large-calibre rifle from the rack to his left, he turned to Bruce. "Take this, and shoot to kill."

Bruce's eyes widened with surprise and he refused to take the weapon at first.

His boss stared into his eyes with urgency and said, "Bruce, you're the best shot out of all of us. These poachers have to be stopped. You have to do this sometimes when you work out on the savannah. It is all of our responsibility!" Anticipating Bruce's next question, he added, "There will not be any legal repercussions. The government has your back on this one, mate."

Bruce took the rifle timidly and set it to rest on a rail in front of him that was fastened to the top of the Land Rover. He looked back at his boss one last time with an "are-you-sure" expression on his face. His boss gave him a quick nod of approval and Bruce lined up the shot. He chose one of the most exposed poachers and deftly squeezed the trigger. As the poacher fell, Bruce, quite to his own astonishment, felt himself fill with exhilaration rather than the guilt he had been anticipating. Recognising immediately that his reaction had not been an appropriate one, he buried the feelings of excitement deep inside himself and assumed a more thoughtful expression that he reasoned was more befitting the circumstances.

His boss patted him on the shoulder as the other poachers sped out of sight, followed closely by the pursuing Land Rovers. "You did good, son."

Bruce nodded and handed him back the rifle. He sat back on the bench seat, his young heart racing, wearing the same thoughtful look that concealed his secret delight. And that was how Bruce Kelly came to kill his first man.

In the years that followed, Bruce made a name for himself as one of the premier professional hunters in the Okavango Delta. His renowned skill with a rifle brought a much sought-after sense of security to overweight American hunters who knew if their shot did not prove fatal, that it was unlikely they would be able to outrun a distressed and confused wild animal that, in some cases, could be as much as five times their own size and hellbent on revenge. For the first time in his life, Bruce was making decent money, but, his nature not being one to be contented by mere trifles (which was how he referred to his own success), he constantly yearned for more.

One day, while driving the savannah alone and looking for signs of where the animals might be feeding in order to prepare himself for the next day's hunt, Bruce looked into the sky to find the familiar circling of vultures that sometimes indicated poaching. He knew that circling vultures didn't always mean trouble, but the sheer number in the sky implied that whatever they were circling was big and, since the ranch closely monitored all of the big game populations within the property's boundaries, Bruce knew that the cause of death was unlikely to have been natural.

Wondering whether or not he should radio it in, he veered his Land Rover in the direction of the hovering birds to investigate. He wasn't sure exactly why, but he couldn't bring himself to pick up the radio mouthpiece that hung just over his gearshift stick and call in to base camp. He knew that company policy obligated him to, but something else was brewing in the back of his head. Something new. The idea that an opportunity was presenting itself to him in that moment; an opportunity that had not presented itself at any time previously and that he knew he may never have again. He was determined to seize it.

Bruce pulled his large, off-road vehicle to the edge of a clearing where the birds' trajectory had led him and cut the engine in order to avoid drawing attention to himself. He scanned the horizon for anything out of the ordinary and sure enough, there they were, busying themselves in the dismemberment of some large animal, the type of which Bruce could not quite make out from his hiding place. He watched them for a while, wondering how in God's name he would be able to approach them without being shot immediately on sight. These were not the type of people to welcome a stranger with anything other than a well-placed bullet to the head or chest. He sat, hidden in the brush for what seemed like hours, racking his brain for a solution that would not present itself. He knew he was running out of time but was still determined not to miss this opportunity. It was just then that the solution, impossible to derive through his own reasoning, presented itself from a wholly unexpected source.

The crack of the first gunshot caught Bruce so off guard that he staggered and nearly fell off the top of his Land Rover. Recovering himself, he grabbed a pair of binoculars and focused them onto the scrambling group of poachers. He noticed that one of them, covered in blood and looking utterly horrified, had collapsed to his knees and was being quickly forgotten by his comrades in the fray. The next crack seemed to finish the job and the kneeling man fell, face-first, onto the ground and moved no more.

By this time, most who remained uninjured had all drawn up their rifles and taken refuge behind their vehicles, returning fire now in the general direction of their unseen ambushers. Two of the others, however, had been so badly disoriented by the sudden onslaught of gunfire that they had been forced to drop where they stood and take cover behind the partially mutilated body of the animal that they had just killed. Realising that the men were not harmed, and desperately needing the help, the poachers with access to the vehicles drew out even more rifles and threw them to the isolated men, who remained crouched behind the massacred animal, careful not to expose themselves to the constant stream of bullets emanating from the tree line.

Bruce watched the gunfight playing out in front of him. He was fortunate in that his position relative to the trajectory of the bullets from either side, solely as a result of dumb luck, placed him entirely out of harm's way. He was therefore free to observe the scene in relative safety very much as one might observe a tennis match from their seat in the bleachers. His gaze darted from the dead man on the ground to the men positioned behind the trucks and he could tell that their situation was growing more dire with each passing moment.

Probably getting low on ammo, he thought.

He glanced at the two men crouched behind the mass of bullet-riddled body, an animal whose life had been taken unjustly and was now being humiliated further in death by being forced to serve as the refuge of its own murderers. *There is no honour in that*, Bruce thought, and yet he smiled at its terrible irony. He noticed that the two crouched men were no longer firing.

Out of ammo. He knew that this was his chance.

Hopping down from the top seat of the Land Rover with his rifle on his shoulder, Bruce, crouched low so as not to give away his position, made his way swiftly along the edge of the clearing towards the ambushing party that seemed now to have their adversaries pinned. He moved carefully and deliberately, never forgetting that, were he to become careless, he may find himself in the path of a stray bullet from the increasingly desperate hoard of poachers. He moved on, doing his best to keep both the ambushed party and the general vicinity of their still hidden ambushers within his line of sight. Bruce's personal well-being, after all, was always his most important consideration in any endeavour and, though he knew that the opportunity which he was at present pursuing could prove to be lucrative, the air in his lungs had always been worth far more to him than diamonds. After a few more moments of slow but steady progress, Bruce came upon that for which he had been searching.

At the edge of the tree line, with eyes only for the poachers at whom they were directing their fire and nothing else, were two men dressed in soldier's garb that Bruce recognised instantly as that worn by members of the Botswana Defence Force's, or BDF's, anti-poaching unit. He knew that these units were generally comprised of at least four soldiers and began to grow alarmed at the prospect that he may at any moment feel a cold, steel barrel pressed up against his back. Relief came quickly, however, when he noticed the two other soldiers, apparently felled by the poachers' return fire, lying motionless at the feet of their brothers-in-arms. Bruce could not believe his luck. Here he was, unseen and with half the work done for him already. He raised his rifle to his shoulder with the calm, collected composure of an experienced hunter, took aim and let out a slow exhale as he squeezed the trigger twice. The shooting died away just as the last bits of life left through the groans and sputterings of the fallen BDF soldiers. And then all was silent. Bruce stood above them, unmoved as always, his rifle barrel still smoking.

He waited patiently, mastering his nerve, for what he knew was coming next. He watched as the confused poachers slowly lowered their weapons, unaware as to why the shooting had ceased. After a few uncertain glances exchanged between one another, they emerged nervously from their cover with rifles raised once again so as not to be taken by surprise should this prove to be some sort of trick. They approached the area from where the bullets, which they had been certain would bring their end, had been pouring forth only moments before.

When they reached the tree line, the first thing they saw was the four BDF soldiers on the ground, but rather than relieve them, this only confused them more. They knew that it was possible, perhaps even likely, that they had hit one or two of them when they had returned fire, but it was impossible that they had managed all four, especially at a moment during which their ammo supply had become so dangerously low that they had all but ceased firing in order to establish a plan of action for once the bullets ran out completely. Yet here they were. Four BDF soldiers, undeniably and irrefutably dead. The poachers let the barrels of their rifles drop a little, apparently ready to accept their good fortune and move on with it, until a voice broke the silence and sent them reeling all over again.

"That was a close one. Eh, fellas?"

The poachers, shocked initially into a frenzy with the unexpected pronouncement but recomposing themselves quickly, focused their sights on a man whom they had not noticed until that moment and began yelling amongst each other in some language that Bruce could not identify. After all, the tribes of Africa had so many languages, and people rarely poached within the borders of their native countries, so he could not be expected to have come into contact with them all.

The wary poachers stared at Bruce in utter disbelief but did not fire their weapons. They seemed almost moved into inaction by his daring. Bruce had anticipated this, or at least he had hoped for it. He was not in a BDF uniform and his rifle was slung, unthreateningly, over his right shoulder. He knew that these precautionary measures might just give him the chance he needed to explain himself, before they had any opportunity of arriving at the undesirable conclusion that it was best that he be disposed of straight away, rather than be given a chance to explain his presence there. Bruce stood perfectly still, not saying anything further, thinking that it was best to let them process the information and arrive at the inevitable realisation that he must be a friend rather than a threat. Otherwise, how had they been saved? When he was satisfied that he was free of any immediate danger he spoke again.

"You fellas are lucky I came along. It didn't look to me like you guys were winning the fight." The stunned poachers, apparently not over the shock of all this, gaped at him with their mouths open. Bruce went on, smiling slightly now. "Don't I even get a thank you?"

After a few minutes, during which it became abundantly clear that this man's motives were not those of a law-abiding citizen, the poachers began to relax. They lowered their weapons and scrutinised the white man who had saved them, something none of them were very accustomed to. Everyone present understood the urgency for speed given that backup forces for the deceased BDF soldiers were undoubtedly already on the way, either because the fallen men had failed to check in with their superiors in order to report success, or because other parties randomly in the vicinity had heard the gunshots and made the decision to render aid of their own volition. Whatever the reason, it was certain that they were coming, and whatever was happening here had to be concluded quickly.

"Who are you?" asked one of the poachers that Bruce took to be the leader. "Why did you kill these men?"

Bruce looked down at the dead men on the ground and then back up to the man who had asked the question. "They would have killed you, and I wanted to speak to you first. Glad to hear that your English is up to scratch! I'm not much for those tribal languages."

The poacher glared suspiciously at Bruce but said nothing.

Bruce continued, "I've been watching you lot, trying to think of a way to talk to you without getting shot first. I knew that if I just walked out of the trees and said 'hello' that you would probably reply by putting a bullet in my head. Then when the BDF came down on you I knew I had a chance here to show you that I was a friend. And now here we are, all friendly, like."

Bruce smiled. The poacher, still looking serious and mistrustful, replied, "And what is it that you wanted with us?"

Bruce's smile faded and his face became serious. "I want a piece of the action, is all. There's a lot more money in what you do than there is for me in what I do. And I'm looking for a change. I just need to get a foot in the door with the right circles and I reckon you guys can put me in touch with the right sort."

Since there was no time for further interrogation, and the white man had saved his and his men's lives, the leader agreed to make the introductions that would help bring Bruce into the trade. They made plans to meet the following week in Maun, thinking that the bustle of Botswana's tourism capital would be useful in concealing their purposes, where certain introductions would be made to various dealers of illegal merchandise who might be interested, should Bruce prove successful in procuring for them something of value.

It was further explained that the means of harvesting and transporting an animal or its valuable pieces for trade were entirely the responsibility of the harvester. This was not union labour, after all, and resources in helping one to make a name for oneself simply did not exist. There was not a support network in this business. You were on your own out there and you needed to know that before going in.

The two men finished their negotiations and then Bruce asked, "What should I call you?"

"James," said the lead poacher curtly, turning his back to him.

Bruce thought that, as far as fake names went, this guy certainly wasn't trying very hard, but, he also knew that it was not uncommon for African natives to adopt Western names when dealing with white folk, and so he said, "Well then, I'll see you in Maun, James."

James nodded and signalled for his men to get back to the trucks. They mounted and sped off in a cloud of whirling dust, leaving Bruce alone at the scene of the crime.

He went back to his own vehicle and, at long last, grabbed the mouthpiece of his radio, pressed the button on the side and said, "Bruce to base camp. We've got a poaching situation on the south-east quadrant of Tract #234. One dead bull elephant, tusks missing, no sign of any poachers. Four dead BDF soldiers and fresh tread marks heading south-east. We're going to need a team out here. Over."

To Bruce's great surprise, James turned out to be a man of his word and on the previously agreed upon date and time, the two men met in Maun exactly as they had planned. Whether it was gratitude that led James to keep his word or some unwritten code of those in the trade, Bruce did not care. His eyes lit up like a child's as they met with James's various black-market contacts, and the true potential of his new enterprise hit him in full force. After a long day of introductions, James, feeling as though his debt had now been repaid in full, bid farewell to the bright-eyed Bruce and left his life forever.

Bruce, pulsating with ambition at his new prospects, barely even noticed him leave. He had never been one whose affection carried beyond the period during which he perceived someone to be useful in the fulfilment of his own selfish desires. And so, immediately following the glorious day in Maun and with a heart full of new ambition, Bruce returned to work on the ranch, this time not to guide hunts but to harvest animals.

For the next year or so, Bruce would operate secretly and successfully out of his post as professional hunter on the ranch. He would venture out alone, harvest an animal and then, in order to throw off any suspicion that he himself might be the true culprit, lament publicly that he had not been able to reach the scene of the crime in time to either apprehend or dispose of the guilty parties.

So convincing was this spectacle that soon his superiors began to suspect that the overwhelming demands of the job were finally getting to him and explained one evening that they were thinking of putting him on administrative duty for the time being in order to grant him a much needed and well-deserved reprieve from the horrors of the savannah. It was only after his sincere and numerous protestations that they relented, but from that time on, he dialled back the severity of his charade so as not to excite such concerns in the future.

Bruce operated precisely thus for some time and with impunity, until his constant failure to arrive at a crime scene in time to intercept the guilty parties began to arouse suspicion amongst the other ranch personnel. Unfortunately for Bruce, prior to his own life of crime, he had been quite adept at not only intercepting poachers but also disposing of them in the manner recommended by the unspoken rules that governed all of the nation's gamekeepers in Botswana. His sudden inability to achieve what he had formerly been the very best at certainly seemed to point an accusatory finger in his direction, and the problem was that now others were starting to pay attention. Realising that time was running out for him, Bruce departed the ranch which had become his first real home. He fled in the dead of one steamy night for places unknown, without so much as a note of goodbye to the folks who had given him so much. And once he had gone, no one would ever see Bruce Kelly in Botswana again.

The next few years found Bruce all over the dark continent. He remained in the illustrious trade of illegal animal parts, such as elephant tusk and rhino horn, but had also expanded his operation to include the smuggling of exotic species for zoos and private estates, as well as fighting animals for underground gambling rings. His smuggling network in the central African nations grew so sophisticated over the next few years that it wasn't long before he had amassed an impressive client list that spanned six of the world's seven continents.

For a long time, Bruce lived the good life, and never once did he regret the decision he'd made back in his ranch days to shed the constraints of law in order to achieve financial success. Then, on one fateful day, something happened that would change everything, and Bruce, pursued by authorities that he knew would not relent until he was captured or dead, was forced to flee his native homeland forever.

Everything had been going largely to plan, which in itself was a rarity for an industry in which unforeseen obstacles were to be expected, and Bruce was overseeing the finishing touches on a shipment worth an estimated £120,000 that was to be smuggled via a well-trodden route through Nigeria, and then on to various destinations around the globe.

Much later he would think to himself that he should have known something was wrong when nothing had gone wrong. It had been too easy up until that point, which should have been a red flag. And then, it had all happened so fast. All of a sudden, it seemed like everything went wrong at the same time. There were soldiers, police and what even looked like armed civilians coming from every direction, closing in on Bruce's men. He watched as some of his men surrendered without resistance and were cuffed while others ran for it or tried to fight. A few of them were gunned down by men who simply had no desire or good reason to run after them. Bruce, snapping back to his senses in the first few moments of the ambush, ran as fast and as far as he could, expecting to feel the sting of a bullet hit him from behind at any moment. He never looked back, however, and never felt a sting. He just ran, faster and faster, his lungs burning as he attempted to draw enough breath to power his failing muscles.

When he finally stopped, he was by the ocean. Still moving briskly, but allowing himself to recover a bit, he made his way along the beach until he reached a small and relatively unknown port just outside of Lagos. He asked around at the various docked vessels and when he found a ship that was preparing to depart for Buenos Aires within the hour, he bribed one of its crewmembers to sneak him onboard as a stowaway.

For what seemed like an eternity but was later discovered to have been just over a week, Bruce hid on the ship, cramped, unwashed and without proper quarters, being fed only sporadically by the mildly concerned crewman that had smuggled him aboard. Once again, he had made a narrow escape, but this time, he knew that there was no going back.

When he finally disembarked in Buenos Aires and paid his accomplice the rest of what he owed for his safe passage, Bruce immediately sought out a private room where he might get his bearings and figure out what to do next.

It wasn't long before he came upon an old ramshackle hotel near the docks and checked himself in. He did not stay there long, however, and, after allowing himself the luxury of a long and desperately needed shower, he set out again in search of a computer. When he finally found one in his hotel's shabby lobby, Bruce went straight for the world news, knowing that the scope of the smuggling bust was such that it would likely warrant international attention. He was right. Plastered all over every news source he could find were headlines related to the "Great Smuggling Ring Bust". He chose an article at random and scanned its pertinent info. Then he opened another and did the same. After a few more articles the full picture came together in his head.

We never had a chance, he thought to himself.

The authorities had been watching them from the start and had waited patiently until all the pieces had lined up so they could take down the whole thing in one fell swoop. The months-long operation had been coordinated across four nations by various activist groups and governments all working cooperatively and without jurisdictional limitations. Bruce was blown away by the scale of it. How had they been able to implant so many of their own men within his smuggling network? The articles read as if they had had people at every level and involved in every step of the process. In the end, the seized merchandise had amounted to 150kg of polished ivory, seventeen turtle shells, three rhinoceros nose horns, one thousand live African parrots, five chimpanzees, 50kg of cocaine that Bruce had not even been aware of and one living baby hippopotamus that held the distinction of being the single most valuable piece in the entire haul. In addition to the enormous inventory seized, twenty-two of Bruce's men had been arrested, as had two unlucky police officers who had accepted bribes in exchange for turning a blind eye.

Quite a bust, thought Bruce before closing the browser window and heading back up to his room to start his new life. *Quite a bust indeed.*

- I I -

Bruce Kelly sat in Proust, sipping a coffee that had long since gone cold. The last bits of humanity that he had still possessed when he arrived in the Americas all those years ago, cramped on a stinking ship, had long since been eroded away by hardship to the point where things like a warm cup of coffee no longer mattered to him. Nothing mattered to him now.

He drank the coffee only because it had caffeine, and since he had grown lethargic with age and disappointment over the years, he needed the artificial jolt of energy. He thought back to his time in Buenos Aires. It hadn't lasted long. He'd fed himself grifting until he'd put enough aside to head north, thinking that he could get started in his old business by exploiting the bountiful species of the Amazon.

He'd had some luck with that and still kept a small operation going in Brazil while he travelled around elsewhere. He'd dabbled briefly in the cocaine trade in Colombia, inspired, it would seem, by the secret entrepreneurial aspirations of his former smuggling subordinate in Africa, and then cock-fighting in Mexico, but neither pursuit had appealed much to him.

He was just back from Jaco, Costa Rica, where he had been looking into the possibility of purchasing a casino, when one of his young lieutenants had delivered a newspaper article to him about a zoo in Georgia that was being revitalised to the unanimous delight of the surrounding townspeople. The article had caught his eye and he'd felt the old familiar spark of ambition, a relic of the Bruce that had existed twenty years ago but had been absent ever since, well up inside himself once more. It appeared that this crumbling zoo, though hardly up to the task, still housed an impressive diversity of rare animal species, all of which were seemingly vulnerable given the lack of structural integrity, funds, security or personnel present at the derelict establishment.

He just needed to act fast, before all those problems were fixed. Wearing a smile that quickly exhausted the muscles of his face, they having long since atrophied from disuse, Bruce immediately abandoned his absurd idea of becoming a casino owner in some burned-out beach town and set about straight away in preparation for his upcoming trip to the United States.

He took another big swig of the cold coffee and glanced at the door.

Still not here yet.

He looked down at his wristwatch.

Late.

He drained the rest of his coffee with the next gulp and signalled the waitress for a refill. The first of the three men that he had been waiting for entered the shop just as the waitress had started pouring and, seeing him come in, Bruce indicated for her to stop and leave him directly.

The man sat down across from Bruce, exhaling a deep sigh and looking around, then said, "Dougie and Mike?"

"Not here yet," replied Bruce, a note of irritation in his voice.

"Are you going to tell us why you brought us here at least, Bruce?"

"As soon as Dougie and Mike get here, Rand, you'll know. We need to give them a few minutes."

Bruce took another protracted gulp from his coffee and kept his focus on the door. Rand, rolling his eyes at the seriousness and mystery of his confidant, looked around for a waitress so that he could order himself a cup of coffee. Unfortunately for Rand, unaware as he was that his friend had just shooed the poor girl away with coldness and that she was now deliberately avoiding the table, he found himself unable to get her attention.

Rand waved his hand wildly in her direction for a few more seconds and then, giving up the effort, yelled across the shop, "Miss, can I get some coffee over here?"

The waitress blushed, evidently confused as to why she had been sent away only to be immediately summoned back, but brought him a cup anyway. As she approached the table, Rand ran a scrutinising gaze up and down her youthful figure. He was careful to do this in a way that would be deliberately obvious to her and when she set the cup down in front of him, he reached for it quickly before she had a chance to pull away so that he could softly graze the tips of her innocent fingers with his own deviant ones.

Rand Patrick had grown up in a sad circumstance, constantly made fun of for his abnormal appearance and, now that he had lived so long that his loneliness had been replaced entirely by hatred, he used the way he looked as a means of making people, whom he perceived to be secretly judging him at all times, uncomfortable. He knew that his bulging eyes, bloodshot these days due to a fondness for drink, and protuberant nose, riddled with burst capillaries for the same reason, were things he could use as his armour rather than his handicap, and he had vowed long ago never again to be a victim.

To sum him up, if, in a single heart, one could combine an unshakeable belief that one will never be able to procure companionship (at least by any means that might be considered normal in the view of civilised society), an insatiable lust and a vengeful desire to revisit the pain of one's own life upon others, then one could readily see how it is that Rand Patrick had come to be the man he was.

"Thank you, sweetheart," said Rand, smiling up at her suggestively and winking.

The waitress shuddered and walked away, not looking back.

He followed her with his immoral gaze for a while until he heard Bruce say, "They're here."

At that moment, the door to Proust flew open with a force that greatly exceeded what would have been necessary to accomplish the task, and two large men, both apparent strangers to the locals gathered inside the coffee shop, entered. The door was flung open with such unrestrained enthusiasm that it threw an unlucky waiter off-balance and sent a tray of empty coffee mugs toppling to the floor where they shattered, greatly intensifying the effect that the slamming door had produced on the collective patrons of the shop.

Bruce shook his head with disgust. That was just what they needed. Attention. The two men, both wearing expressions that made it look as though they had entered the shop by accident, glanced around and, finding Bruce and Rand at long last, joined them at their table. Bruce waited for the conversation at the other tables, which had ceased in the wake of the dramatic entrance, to resume before he spoke.

"Bloody morons," was the first thing he was able to say through gritted teeth. "We don't want to be drawing attention to ourselves and you roll in here like bloody stampeding buffalo."

The two men exchanged nervous glances and then said together, "Sorry, boss."

From there, Dougie took the thread and added, "We weren't sure we were in the right place."

To see Dougie and Mike together, one might naturally assume that they were brothers. They were both made of the same raw material, and a prolonged time spent in each other's company had coevolved in each of them the same mannerisms and vocal inflections. They were both enormous in size and lacking in wit.

They were, as might be assumed with regard to those who were in possession of their unique set of skills, the *muscle*. Goons for hire. Possessing just enough intelligence to carry out an order successfully, but not enough to question the validity or necessity of that order. They were perfect for the purpose that they served because the simplicity of their intellect meant that they were not bothered with the morality or legality, things that sometimes plagued loftier minds, of the tasks with which they were charged, nor did they even entirely understand them. Being thus ignorant of their own potential baseness, they were completely untouched by the remorse that often came to haunt those in similar lines of work. On the contrary, they slept with the tranquillity of the innocent every night as soon as they found their beds.

It was Mike who was next to speak but, having nothing of his own to say, he merely echoed what his friend had said immediately before him: "Yeah, boss. We just wasn't sure. Couldn't find a sign or nothing."

Bruce closed his eyes in meditation, attempting to beat back the anger welling up inside him. Mike and Dougie looked concernedly at Rand, who shrugged, and then back at each other. After a few more moments of silence, Bruce's eyeballs made an appearance once more, revealing that the storms which had been building behind them had now cleared. The table let out a collective sigh of relief and then all present focused the entirety of their combined attentions on Bruce, feeling now that the time had finally come for the big reveal as to what had brought them to this sleepy town in Georgia.

Bruce glanced around the café one last time to make sure that all of the conversations surrounding them had resumed, and then at each of them in turn, almost as if trying to build up the suspense for dramatic effect, and said finally, "Alright, listen up. Here's what we're gonna do…"

-III-

GINNY'S FATHER WAS IN AN EXCEEDINGLY GOOD MOOD AS he waited for his daughter to arrive. It was the eve of his beloved zoo's grand reopening and everything had been planned to perfection. The last few weeks leading up to this moment had been labour-intensive and stressful for all involved parties, but they had also been among the most joyous of the old man's long life.

After countless years spent feeling powerless in the face of a perceived need to kill in order to maintain his own survival, he was now realising his dream of building a sanctuary in which life was to be protected rather than destroyed. He of course knew that success in this endeavour would not forgive the innumerable sins of his past, but he also knew that when one finds him or herself confronted with the predicament of being unable to achieve the ultimate goal of their heart, there is reward in the toil all the same and the endeavour remains worth seeing through to its end. In addition to the peace afforded the old man by the zoo's having turned him from wolf into shepherd, there was still further reason for the exceptional mood that he had been enjoying as of late.

It was the marked change in Ginny that brought him the most joy of all. Though she was always happy, she had now blossomed into a creature of such enviable glee that the whole of the town, who had always loved her enormously even as she had been, basked in her radiance and even absorbed it themselves. Like a contagion of light, her warmth permeated the hearts of the whole town and everyone, crediting the zoo as the sole driver of the change in the young girl's life, seemed to be marking their calendars for the big day on which it would finally reopen its doors after so many years spent in darkness, and deliver happiness at last to the weary townspeople.

The old man was standing at a front window when he saw Ginny skipping up the sidewalk with, as was always the case these days, Ainsley Blake close at her heels. His lips curled involuntarily into the familiar smile that was always present whenever he was in close proximity to his daughter, and he turned to make his way down to the front door in order to meet them as they approached.

Beaming, he swung the door open before they had a chance to knock and, stooping as always to kiss Ginny, he said, "Glad to see you two! Big day tomorrow!"

The three of them stood in the doorway for a few moments smiling at each other, an action Blake seemed to have at last grown accustomed to after years spent wearing a perpetual look of indifference, and then, following Ginny's lead, the two men turned and pursued her into the house.

Upon entering the atrium, Ginny sped off on a direct path to the study where they always conducted their zoo-related business, leaving the two men behind and quite alone together. Her father, though he had long since acknowledged Blake's quality and accepted his status as boyfriend to his only daughter, had found that in the wake of their discussion and the shameless pleas with which he had berated him on Ginny's behalf, he couldn't help but feel a bit awkward whenever alone with Blake.

After all, a man like him had never been in a position to have to plead his case to anyone. On the contrary, he had spent his life perched atop the zenith of every circumstance, unchallenged, and it was to him that cases were pleaded, their outcomes depending solely upon his judgement.

It had therefore been an uncomfortable and unfamiliar reversal of position when he had found himself grasping the hands of Ainsley Blake and begging for his word that Blake would protect the daughter whom he loved more than all else in the world.

Unsurprisingly, Blake had sensed the old man's awkwardness immediately following their confrontation, and rather than thwart it by making it apparent that he was perfectly comfortable on his end with regard to the matter, which might have rendered the old man's embarrassment inert, he instead became infected with it himself. Now, though it was indeed rare that they ever found themselves together without Ginny present, they were wholly unable to converse in the slightest degree, and so were forced to make fast excuses whenever necessary in order to rejoin her as quickly as possible. In keeping with this unspoken pact, the two men gave each other quick nods of consent that showed them to be in agreement and continued on to the study in search of the only one that could assuage their discomfort. She, whom they both loved.

When they entered the study, they found Ginny already happily absorbed in documents that outlined some portion of the next day's plan. Her father smiled down at her, his heart full of gratitude at this proof of his daughter's unwavering diligence in an endeavour so dear to him, and one that he had rightly believed her to have had very little interest in herself. Her dedication was a proof of her love for him, which he recognised with pride. The old man turned to Blake and indicated for him to sit down before lightly pulling the papers from Ginny's hand and setting them on the table by her side. Ginny and Blake, both correctly perceiving that the old man wished to say something to the room at large, remained silent and focused on him, listening.

Ginny Harrison's father was not a man to allow emotions to get the better of him. When she was a little girl, she had often misinterpreted his stoicism as a lack of concern, but now as an adult, she admired that he was able to master his impulses with such apparent ease.

She thought him more evolved than most in that he was not at the mercy of his baser instincts. She had learned with age that the emotions of mankind are often aroused at the expense of more desirable qualities like rationality, intelligence and prudence. The higher thinking of man and the barbaric impulses of the animals over which we claim dominance cannot survive simultaneously in a single human form. Instead, when one is present it is only because it has supplanted the other until, given enough time or some counteracting stimulus, the latter will be supplanted by the former once more. Ginny's father's emotion never won out over his reason and this was what she so admired. However, as she watched him standing before them and trying to speak, she could finally see his humanity laid out bare at her feet and beyond his control.

At first it seemed like the old man would be unable to speak. Ginny, being unfamiliar with her father's emotional tells, did not understand and wondered if he could not find the right words. Blake, however, seemed to understand immediately and bowed his head low so as not to risk wounding the old man's damaged pride further by bearing witness to this new demonstration of what others belonging to their kind would undoubtedly label as weakness.

Ginny rose from her seat, her eyes sparkling in solidarity with her father's, and approached him, asking, "What's wrong, Daddy?"

The old man, still without speaking, indicated for her to return to her seat, which she did obediently. Perceiving the effect that he was producing on his audience in the bowed head of Ainsley Blake and sparkling eyes of his daughter, the old man seemed to regain some of his composure.

Taking a long exhale and looking at both of them in turn, he finally began. "I just want to say thank you. Both." He paused again, still looking uncertain as to his own eventual goal in giving this speech, then went on, this time solely to his daughter. "I know you must have thought I was crazy when I told you that I had bought the old zoo. And maybe you were right."

The father and daughter both shared a smile full of fond reminiscence as the old man continued, "But you stuck by me all the way to the end and now we've almost done it. You have helped an old man to achieve his dream and there are no words to express my gratitude."

The emotion that had paralysed the old man threatened him again now, but he powered on, taking her hand. "I have lived a long time, and there were times when I thought that I had no right to happiness. That it would forever elude me and more, that I didn't deserve it even if it were to present itself within my reach. You gave me that happiness that I had no right to seek for myself and I have been determined to be worthy of it ever since the day you were born. Every day since then it has only grown. Now, you have given me that gift all over again in helping me to realise this dream. We have created a sanctuary together and spared all our animals from uncertain fates. Now, I can hope to give to others a small part of what you have given to me, though I could never hope to match the depth of your gift."

Tears streamed from Ginny's eyes as she listened to her father. She had never seen him like this and was quite overcome in the face of something so powerful and unprecedented.

She threw her arms around him and, choking back tears, said, "I love you, Daddy. I would give you all the happiness in the world, even if it meant I had to give up my own. You are the best father a girl could ever have."

The old man wiped an unashamed tear from his eye and then turned to Blake. In the powerful and unmovable eyes of Ainsley Blake the old man just barely perceived a single fledgling tear, migrating uncertainly down a face that had remained unwetted for centuries.

The two men looked at each other in silence for a few minutes and then the old man said simply and sincerely, "Thank you," and reached out to shake Blake's hand.

Blake, in complete awe of everything that had just transpired, held the old man's gaze and took the hand that had been offered him, replying in kind, "No, it is I who thank you."

-IV-

D R HUGO WEGENER SAT IN THE SUNLIT COFFEE SHOP, politely declining the confused waitress's numerous offers to bring him something to eat or drink. He was not hungry, of course, and had only entered the coffee shop for want of anything better to do. For a while he watched the waitress, who appeared unsure as to what company protocol might demand of her in a situation where a table was being occupied by a man who was not, nor did it seem that he ever intended to become, a customer. Growing bored of the minor spectacle that he was causing, Hugo opened his newspaper, as was his daily custom, and began to read it carefully, perusing it for any information that might be of interest to him.

Though he pretended to himself that there were lots of potential stories that could be of use to him, and indeed it was for these that he had always searched over the years, in truth, it was for stories from which he might garner new information, no matter how slight, regarding his estranged friend that he searched now. In the months since his rupture with Ainsley Blake, Hugo had become wholly consumed with melancholy. He did not, after all, have a Ginny Harrison to occupy the hole in his heart that had been left open by the loss of his friend.

When he had arrived in the small Georgian town initially, he had had no intention of staying. For many years preceding that point, he had lived a largely nomadic lifestyle, settling nowhere for any extended period of time. Being always on the move had ensured his safety, because given enough time, the symptoms of his true nature were inevitably manifested beyond what could be reasonably ignored by any single population, and it was to him that those symptoms always led.

When he met Blake, however, the lure of companionship after countless years spent in solitude had been such that he abandoned his strict protocol and resolved instead to take a gamble on happiness.

Ginny's arrival on the scene made him realise instantly that he had been wrong to do so. It was exactly that sort of behaviour that was most dangerous to them, and he felt that he'd had no other choice but to abandon his friend when Blake could not bring himself to abandon the girl. In the weeks following his departure, he had attempted to re-establish his nomadic routine, and had even believed that it would be easy to do so. Unfortunately, the good doctor soon realised that while one might close their heart once in order to shield it from pain, it is not so easy to close it a second time once it has been reopened and allowed again to bind itself to that of another.

After several months spent labouring under a stubborn refusal to succumb to the yearning in his chest, Hugo Wegener had dropped to his knees, cursed the sky and at long last relented.

Hugo was about halfway through his newspaper, growing more comfortable with the passing of each page devoid of any news on Blake, when something called his attention away from the black and white pages. The door to the coffee shop had exploded open with such a large *crack* that it caused the whole of the café to collectively jump out of their seats with fright.

He turned just in time to see an entire tray of empty coffee mugs go crashing to the floor as the stunned waiter who had been carrying them struggled to keep himself upright. Just as suddenly, the bright sunlight that had been streaming in through the open door vanished, eclipsed by the massive forms of two giant men who were now entering the coffee shop with dazed looks on their round and shiny faces. Hugo, along with every other customer present in the small shop, stared, open-mouthed at the leviathans who had executed such a dramatic entrance. All conversation ceased, the waitresses all suspended their rounds and even the consistent hum of porcelain hitting porcelain, common to all coffee shops, faded away into silence. The shop was united in awe of these two strangers and twenty different pairs of eyes followed them to their seats, which creaked unsteadily as they sat, bending precariously under the massive weights of their new occupants.

Hugo Wegener, who, as we know, possessed a somewhat encyclopaedic knowledge of the world, accumulated over countless years and honed by innumerable experiences, took a marked interest, first in the two giant simpletons, and then in those whom they had apparently come to meet at the coffee shop.

He had known many men in the course of his abnormally long life and during that time had become quite proficient in reading the subtle clues of expression on the faces of those whom he was in a position to observe, and then translating accurately the insights which could be gleaned therein.

His keen eyes darted around the table, and he could tell immediately and without a doubt that their meeting was to some nefarious end. When his eyes reached the man who looked as though he was the centre towards which the others had directed their focus, he paused. The man looked livid, as though it were costing him a great deal not to start screaming at his tardy and recklessly conspicuous comrades.

Hugo knew that this man must be the leader of the rag-tag group, and that they had chosen this spot as the meeting place where some devious plan would be put into action. When the angry man looked up from his compatriots and around at the tables surrounding them, apparently checking to make sure that they had all shifted their focuses back to their own business and were no longer looking towards the two giants, Hugo buried his face back in his paper to avoid detection. His keen ears, however, he kept trained on the foursome. After a few short moments, the group's leader had apparently decided that it was safe to discuss their business and, when at last he opened his mouth, Hugo was ready to hear every word.

-V-

"ARE YOU GUYS READY TO GO?" ASKED THE OLD MAN impatiently as he waited by the front door.

Scuttling noises from inside the house that did not appear to be growing any louder told him that he would likely be waiting for some time longer. The morning had been full of tenderness and emotion in anticipation of the zoo's grand opening, and the father, daughter and he, who was once an outsider but had since become like family during the course of the preceding months, all felt accordingly drained. It was Ginny who had been most affected by the profusion of gratitude and feeling that had dominated the morning, because whereas each of the two men had but one to whom they directed their sentiments, she had two, both of whom she felt deserved an equal share of her heart.

Recognising her fatigue, both men set about immediately in preparing a hearty lunch in order to restore her strength, for the day ahead of them remained long. Ginny ate with relish and, as is often the case when one is at the same time hungry, jovial and in good company, failed to notice the plates of food that remained untouched in front of each of the men. After lunch, the group took to a sitting room in order to have an hour or two of repose before setting out again. Only a few minutes had elapsed before Ginny was happily dozing, deep in the restorative sleep of one whose mind is at total peace and wants for nothing.

The two men, though not sleeping, remained completely quiet throughout the duration of the nap so as not to disturb the sleeping girl. This arrangement greatly benefitted both men, as it provided an excellent excuse for avoiding the awkwardness that an attempted conversation would have undoubtedly produced. After a little more than an hour had passed, Ginny awoke of her own accord, refreshed and grateful to have re-entered the waking world to the smiling faces of the two people that she loved most of all.

Her father had been first to stand and, doing so, he said to his daughter, "You're looking refreshed."

"I feel refreshed," said Ginny, stretching. "I didn't actually mean to fall asleep. But I guess sometimes a good nap is just what you need! Seems like I must've needed it at least."

Her father smiled and then checked his watch, saying, "Well, I'm glad because we need to get going now."

"Oh, it's time already? How long was I asleep? Oh, who cares, I'm ready!" said Ginny excitedly, jumping up from the couch on which she'd been napping.

"Yes, it's time," said the old man, chuckling. "I'm going to go change and I will meet you two at the front door in five minutes."

Ginny moved in on her father and planted a kiss on his cheek before turning to Blake, grabbing his hand and leading him out of the room. Calling back to her father, she said, "Okay. See you in five minutes!"

When Blake and Ginny finally got to the front door, they found the old man already waiting there, wearing a mock scowl and tapping the face of his wristwatch accusatorily.

Ginny laughed and said, "Give me a break. It's been six minutes tops."

"Six and a half minutes, actually," said the old man with a smile.

Ginny rolled her eyes as her father opened the front door and indicated for them to go ahead. Once they had crossed the threshold into the front yard, he followed them, turning to lock the door behind himself.

"I'm so excited!" said Ginny as her father fell into stride beside her and the group of three exited the old man's yard onto the public sidewalk. "I just can't believe it's finished!"

"And I can't wait for you to see it," replied the old man. "You're not even going to recognise it! When was the last time you went over there anyway?"

"Can't remember. Anyway, I can't wait to see what it looks like!" she said, walking so fast that her father had to quicken his step so as not to fall behind.

Blake, on the other hand, allowed himself to lag behind a bit so that he could observe. Being accustomed to silence, he always preferred to enjoy the interactions of the father and daughter from the perspective of a spectator rather than that of a participant. Their bond was something that he coveted and he did not wish to intrude upon it.

Their mutual admiration and the depth of their respect for one another had struck a chord with him in its remoteness, but also in its familiarity. Though the bond that their connection reminded him of had not been of blood, he still remembered fondly the adopted father that he had loved and lost so many years ago whenever he observed them together. Over the past few months, Blake had slowly been allowing himself to believe in the possibility of his own happy ending after so many years of seemingly unbreachable darkness. He allowed himself to take as a sign that reassuming the only name by which he had ever known happiness had indeed delivered it to him once more. Watching the happy family of two now walking at a near jog in front of him, he thought of the great Lord Blake and took the similar paternal bond shared between Ginny and her father as a further proof of his good fortune.

163

Exiting the residential street on which stood her father's house, Ginny lead the group onto the town's main drag. It was early in the afternoon and the street was mostly deserted, since it was both the hottest time of the day and a time during which most found themselves obliged to work rather than meander around town at their leisure. The group therefore walked and talked freely, not bothering to keep their voices down or stay within the borders of the sidewalk. They continued merrily in this fashion for a few blocks, laughing and spilling into the street, until they heard a harsh and apparently frustrated voice emanate from some shadowy side alley.

"I thought you said it was right here, Mike?"

A different, but equally harsh, voice responded, this one on the defensive. "How the hell am I supposed to know where it is? I've never been here before! I said it was around here somewhere."

Ginny, her father and Blake all stopped in their tracks and stared in the direction of the disembodied voices that had intruded so unexpectedly on their frivolity. Whoever they were, they were clearly not from around here.

After another minute, the owners of the two voices appeared out of their darkened alley and emerged into the sunlit street. They were the two biggest men that Ginny had ever seen and were, in fact, so large that they could have even been counted among the biggest ever seen by the two men whose longevity had permitted them to see so much. The threesome watched in silence as the two men argued, wandering uncertainly down the sidewalk, apparently in search of some address with which they were unfamiliar but at which they were expected.

Ginny watched most attentively of all and when one of the men finally stopped in front of a door, casting his gaze back and forth between the sign above it and a piece of paper in his hand, seemingly lost in the midst of some great calculation that exceeded his abilities, Ginny whispered so that only the two others could hear, "That's Proust."

The large man, seeming at last to decide that he had indeed located their correct destination, called to his counterpart, "Dougie, I think I found it. Right here."

The one called Dougie approached, reached out a single enormous hand and gave a great pull. The door, however, did not budge. Still not noticing the boldface sign on the door that read "PUSH" in all caps, Dougie gave the door another aggressive but ineffective tug, then stepped back, scratching his head in confusion. The other man, pocketing the piece of paper on which Ginny was certain the address had been written, walked up to the entrance, and at the exact moment that his friend had decided upon the same course of action, the two hulking giants both simultaneously put their massive shoulders into the small door, which they had regrettably mistaken as stuck closed, and pushed with the full power of their combined might. The lightweight panel of wood and glass flew open so violently in response to this unprecedented use of force that the two nearly tumbled into the shop over each other.

Ginny stifled a laugh as she watched the spectacle. Her father and Blake both looked suspicious but assumed smiles in order to match her reaction.

"Have you ever seen men that big?" asked Ginny, still on the verge of laughter. "Where do you think they came from?"

"Just out-of-towners," answered her father.

"I hope they didn't kill anybody when that door flew open," said Ginny with affected concern.

All three of them laughed, and then her father spoke again, trying to refocus them all on the original object of their outing, which had been forgotten in the wake of the two herculean strangers. "Come on, let's keep going."

Ginny recomposed herself and soon they were walking again, the father and daughter side by side, and the lover tagging along behind them.

When they finally arrived at the magnificent gates of the impossible zoo, they paused for a moment before entering so as to savour the moment. It was a triumph. Glorious, and against all odds. Ginny could not believe that the venture she had once taken to be a sign of dementia in her ageing father was now here in front of her, real, in all its pride and majesty.

"It looks beautiful, Daddy," said the girl, attaching herself firmly to her father's strong arm. "I am so proud of you. All of us."

The old man patted her hand affectionately as he stared up at the zoo's freshly painted sign with glistening eyes.

He separated from her, and, extending his hand towards the zoo in invitation, said with a smile, "Shall we then?"

-VI-

THE TRANSFORMATION THAT THE DERELICT ZOO HAD undergone was beyond anything that could have been imagined. The landscaping was sharp and fresh, just as man always intends before nature has its ultimate say and pushes back, through drought or weed, against the artificial boundaries that have been imposed upon it. The paths were smooth, uncracked and, indeed, brand new in many places where the broken concrete had been unsalvageable. Fresh paint sparkled from every direction, and the rusty metal bars that had once donned the cages of the past had all been replaced with safety glass and barrier moats that offered a more visitor-friendly, unrestricted view of the animals as they went about their daily lives. The zoo's main path, on which Blake, Ginny and her father now walked, would serve to guide visitors from the entrance and through the zoo in optimal fashion, taking guests by each exhibit that the zoo offered without exception. There were bathrooms and concession stands as well, all placed at strategic intervals along the trail, fully equipped and ready to accept the guests that tomorrow promised to bring. The trio, taking this all in, did not have to walk long before they arrived at the first enclosure of their tour containing a mischievous-looking band of capuchin monkeys.

"I thought these guys would be good for the first encounter," said the old man, gazing fondly at the tiny, capering animals. "Everyone recognises these little guys. They're familiar, and I think that's important for people to identify with when they arrive here for the first time. It will bring them comfort and also a good laugh. I knew they would be a crowd favourite the second I set eyes on them back when I first bought the place."

The old man approached the enclosure slowly so as not to alarm the monkeys, and said quietly, but in a cartoonish voice that did not suit him, as one who is normally very serious might speak to a human baby, "But you guys have gotten quite an upgrade since then, haven't you?" When the monkeys failed to respond to his question, he turned back to Blake and Ginny, chuckling to himself, and said, "Yes, everyone likes the capuchins. Shall we go on?"

Ginny and Blake exchanged a look of bewildered amusement at the childlike wonderment now present in the old man's character, but said nothing and followed excitedly, eager to watch this change in him play out as they continued down the trail.

"So, how many species do we have here total?" asked Ginny, catching up to her father.

"Three hundred and fifty," replied the old man. Then, before she could respond, he added proudly, "But over one thousand individual animals."

Ginny nodded, genuinely impressed, as they approached the bird sanctuary. The bird sanctuary was an enormous mesh tent in which a multitude of different species all lived in harmony. It was Ginny's father's ambition to put all of the zoo's birds within this structure, thinking naively that it would be the most enjoyable circumstance for them to live in relative freedom together. In the end, however, he had been forced to separate some due to the predatory nature of their species, and others simply because of the overall capacity of the giant mesh enclosure. It was, after all, of paramount importance to the old man that the animals of the zoo be treated with as much respect, dignity and competency as possible, and that meant that sometimes an original idea had to be abandoned in the face of compelling evidence against it.

After a few more stops along the trail, and some excited impromptu chats with the various zoo staffers that they had met along the way, Ginny declared that she required a visit to the ladies' room.

Turning in the direction of the nearest facility, she left the two men behind her, saying simply, "Don't let me keep you guys. Keep going and I will catch up in a little bit. I want to talk to some more of the staffers. They all look so excited!"

Once she had disappeared completely into one of the nearby restrooms, the old man turned to Blake with a serious expression that was oddly out of keeping with the overall mood of the happy afternoon, and said, "Mr Blake. I'm glad that you and I have a moment together. Now that we are alone, I would like to show you something. Come with me, please, if you would."

Blake, unsure as to what exactly the old man could possibly want with him, nevertheless did as he was instructed and allowed himself to be led further down the path.

They passed several enclosures without stopping before finally reaching a large arching sign that straddled the path and indicated that they were about to enter the "Cats of Africa" exhibit. Blake entered beneath the archway and found himself surrounded by countless animals that together represented what seemed like every single species of great predatory cat native to the infamous Dark Continent. There were majestic lions, undisputed kings of the savannah. A pair of leopards, one spotted and one jet-black, with fur so beautiful that they were undoubtedly the envy of all the others. There was a serval looking almost domestic, and a caracal looking as though it were the pride of extinct pharaohs. Blake took in the sight, moved by the majesty of the animals. There had been a cheetah at one point, too, he knew, but the old man had long since sent it to live on a preserve in Texas after deciding that keeping a creature capable of achieving such stunning speed confined to an enclosure in which it would be unable to ever fully achieve that potential, was tantamount to a crime against nature.

Neither man spoke for a long while, each admiring the craftsmanship of nature as represented in the beautiful apex predators.

It was the old man who finally broke the silence, "Of all the world's many creatures, I have always loved the large cats most of all." He turned his eyes from the cats to Blake, who returned his gaze, and then went on. "It is well known that it is the natural instinct of these animals to kill their prey swiftly, but without mercy, so that they might survive. Such is the way of nature, now and always."

The old man paused, glancing again around the cages and then focusing once more on Blake, who was understandably confused as to the point that was trying to be made. He had the impression that the old man was searching for the right words to properly convey his message in a manner that was in keeping with the importance that he seemed to attach to it.

After a few short moments, the old man appeared to have found them, and continued, "It is the privilege of a beast that it may kill without remorse, without consequence, without evil. So we, who possess the intellect of our higher being, build these impenetrable cages so that their unassuageable instinct to kill cannot do us any harm. But, it is not just for ourselves that we build the cage; it is for them, too. Without the safety of the cage that we have provided for them, their natures would inevitably bring about their own end. We cage the beast so that they cannot hurt us, as would be their natural way, and we cage the beast so that we will not be forced to hurt them, which would be ours. Because we are not beasts ourselves, we do not have the luxury of neglecting our duty in this. Do you understand?"

The old man's eyes filled with tears as he stared into the unflinching but compassionate eyes of Ainsley Blake.

"Did Ginny ever tell you about her mother?" asked the old man. Blake said nothing, but the look on his face told the old man that she had not, so he continued, "I'm not surprised. She was just a girl when it happened and doesn't ever speak of it."

The pitiable father let out a long exhale, apparently preparing himself for some miserable tale which it would be very difficult for him to recount. "We were living in a town not far from here; Ginny has always been in Georgia, and I had never known happier times. I had a wife, whom I loved deeply, and though she knew the truth about me, she loved me, too. I still can't imagine why. We had a daughter who was the light of our lives. Ginny. Always happy, never sad, as you well know by now. Unfortunately, I had been careless, thinking that what I was doing under the cover of night had only been so that I could survive, and no other reason.

"I was even using the people that loved me as justification for my actions. I said that it was for them that I had to survive, for them that I had to kill. In short, I behaved exactly as would a beast and I pretended to myself that I had no other recourse but to do so. I didn't really believe that, of course, I just wanted to believe it. It was easier that way.

"We always have a choice, Mr Blake, never forget that.

"It wasn't long before two brothers came looking for me. It seemed that, in the blindness of my bloodlust, I had taken the life of a third brother, the youngest, and now they had come to seek their revenge. I had no right to be surprised. I knew that it was bound to happen someday, no matter how much I tried to convince myself that it wouldn't. Fortunately, Ginny was not home when they came. I am tormented to this day by the guilt of it! By the guilt of knowing that she could have been there were it not for some fortuitous coincidence, and what might have happened to her if she had been. I can't even think about it. I put my own family at risk, Blake!"

The old man wiped his eyes before continuing his story. Blake was frozen to the spot, shocked at what was being revealed to him.

"I was not in the room when they entered it. It was only my wife whom they found there, and though I, the one whom they sought, was absent, they did not show her any mercy. A bullet from one of their pistols found her heart, and she was dead before I was even able to be at her side.

"I reacted instantly, solely out of anger and vengeance, and stuffed my grief deep down inside me for consideration at some later time. I disposed quickly and pitilessly of the two intruders, who, of course, could not have stood a chance against me in spite of what they may have believed when they had first set out that night. After my revenge had been taken, I held my beautiful wife, whom I knew I had killed by my negligence, and vowed to never again lose control.

"I believed, as you can certainly understand after having heard my story, that I would never be happy again, but, as you also well know, Ginny's heart burns with such brightness that one cannot live in proximity to it without becoming infected with its light, no matter how black the darkness that seeks to challenge it. I am asking you, Blake, to swear to me that you will preserve that light."

The father, trembling with the emotion called forth by his story, indicated the fearsome cats surrounding them, and concluded, "We who possess the means of rising above the savagery of our own natures, do not possess the luxury of acting as would a beast. The cages we construct are not just for others but for ourselves."

Blake nodded in deep comprehension and the two men gazed into each other's eyes in mutual understanding. From that moment on, an unspoken bond had been sealed, and could never be undone.

-VII-

"THERE YOU GUYS ARE," SAID AN EXASPERATED-LOOKING Ginny as the two men emerged from the "Cats of Arica" exhibit. "I've been looking all over for you!"

The two men, both masters of their own emotions and therefore no longer wearing on their faces any perceptible trace of what had just transpired between them, walked towards her, looking as though the joyful feeling of the afternoon had proceeded uninterrupted throughout the course of her absence.

Her father was first to address her. "You must not have looked too hard. We never left the path."

"Well, you should have known that I wouldn't stay on the path," she replied with narrowed eyes, but wearing a smile that exposed the truth of her feeling.

Her father, recognising his daughter's familiar charade, smiled back at her and asked, "Been exploring?"

"Just talking," said Ginny, her eyes reassuming their normal size and shape. "Everyone around here seems really excited, Dad. They all think it's going to be incredible tomorrow. What were you guys doing?"

Blake, seizing upon the inclusive nature of this question as

a means to enter the conversation, replied, "Your father was just showing me the African cat exhibit."

"Ah," said Ginny. "They are his favourites. I think he feels some sort of kinship with them, but he denies it." She smiled at her father again and then took Blake's arm, saying, "So, what's next?"

"Well, we've still got more zoo to see," said her father, shrugging his shoulders in a manner that suggested this was obvious. "Let's go!"

The three of them continued on the meandering path throughout the glorious zoo, taking care to stop and inspect every enclosure and brief every employee on the plan for the next day's grand opening. All of the marketing leading up to the big day had been deemed a success, though the next day would be the true standard by which it would ultimately be measured, and word seemed to have spread of its own accord throughout the town. Everything seemed to be pointing to the zoo's opening day being a smash hit. When Ginny's father had inspected every square inch of the zoo and everyone was finally satisfied that supplies were stocked, machinery was fully operational, and safeguard protocols were in place and understood by those responsible for them, the old man at last gave his permission that the group might depart the zoo until the following morning.

The sun hung low in the sky when Ginny and her two men finally exited the zoo's front gate into the parking lot. It had been a long day, full of the kind of emotion that drains a person from deep within their soul in a way that purely physical exertion never could, no matter its intensity. Ginny hung heavily on the arm of Ainsley Blake as the three of them reappeared on the sidewalk on which they had been walking hours before and in the opposite direction. Were it not for this walk, Ginny knew that she would already be asleep, whether at home in bed or in the backseat of a car, and every step seemed to force her to rely more heavily on the strong and unmovable arm of the man she loved. The father, sensing his daughter's need for repose, and Blake, interpreting correctly the steadily increasing weight on his own arm, agreed with a glance to walk directly to Ginny's apartment in place of the old man's house at which they had initially all planned to have dinner.

When they arrived, her father produced a spare key to the front entrance from his pocket and opened the door to admit Blake, who was now very much carrying the dozing young girl, before entering himself. Blake carried her across her front living room and into her bedroom, where he lifted her effortlessly into the bed, pulling a thick quilt over her. When he re-emerged into the living room, he found the father there, waiting to bid him good night.

"She is sleeping like the dead," said Blake, looking sadly reminiscent in the wake of his comment and smiling softly.

"And we are waking as the dead," added the old man, recognising the familiar look in Blake's eye that is common to all who have lost something dear to them which had, prior to losing it, been taken for granted.

"Indeed," replied Blake, still seemingly lost in some melancholy recollection that was, nonetheless, skewed by his present happiness.

Blake walked the old man to the door and opened it.

The old man put his hand out for Blake to shake and said, "You are a good man, Ainsley."

Blake took the hand and shook it slowly and deliberately, answering, "I have lived a very long time. And yet, in a very short time you have taught me much. Your lessons are those that have eluded me all these years in spite of circumstances that should have forced them upon me long ago. It took you to make me see what was right in front of my face. I owe you a great debt of gratitude, not only for the daughter whom you have so graciously entrusted to me, but for the value of your counsel that you have given so freely. If I can hope to be guided by the actions of another throughout whatever remains of my seemingly endless existence, then I hope it is against your actions that I come to measure my own."

Blake ended his speech and released the old man's hand. The two men nodded to each other, signifying their mutual respect, and then the old father exited the apartment as the sun's last rays dropped below the horizon and out of sight, ushering in the night.

-VIII-

I T WAS ALMOST MIDNIGHT WHEN THE PHONE RANG AT Ginny's apartment. She shot up in her bed like a rocket, startled by the sudden loud noise that had called her so abruptly away from her pleasant dreams. At first, she was unaware of what was going on, but as the sleep faded, her mind began to piece together the scene. She was home, but she could barely remember getting there after the zoo. She swung her head around to the clock and saw that it was midnight. The phone was still ringing. It would either ring forever or whoever was on the other side would abandon their attempt and hang up of their own accord since there was no answering machine. Ainsley Blake entered the bedroom just as Ginny's full wits were returning to her.

"Do you want me to turn the ringer off?" he asked, placing himself beside her on the edge of the bed.

"No, don't mute it," said Ginny, apparently thinking hard and fast. "Who would call at this hour? Maybe it's an emergency. I need to answer."

She said this last part with resolve as she excavated herself from underneath the bedcovers and made her way out to the phone in the living room. Fearing that she might miss the call, she neglected to sidestep the pair of shoes that stood on the floor between her and the phone and would have taken a nasty spill had Blake not been miraculously present at her side to catch her before she hit the ground.

Once he had righted her, she moved again towards the phone, popping the receiver deftly out of its cradle and saying, "Yes?" When she did so, it was with a voice that betrayed her disquiet regarding the potential nature of the call.

Blake watched her for any sign as to what might be happening, but she said nothing, apparently listening intently. When her eyes began to dilate in alarm, Blake knew that something was wrong. He did not need to wait for the startled, "Wait, what?!" to confirm his suspicions before he had re-entered the bedroom to gather the shoes and clothing that would be necessary in order to venture back out of the apartment and into the night. When he was once again in the living room, he found Ginny, no longer talking into the phone but instead holding it out to him.

"He wants to talk to you," Ginny said with confusion and worry. "He won't tell me what's going on."

Blake, looking every bit as confused as Ginny, took the phone and said, "Yes?"

It was Ginny's father on the other end, his voice moving rapidly through the information that he needed to convey, motivated by that excitement that instinctively moves men of action during a time of need. It was not fear or helplessness, but purpose, and Ainsley Blake knew it well.

When Blake had finished the unexpected phone call and replaced the receiver back into its cradle, he turned abruptly to find himself face to face with Ginny. She wore a look of concern that Blake could tell was really a command that he reveal the truth of her father's late-night call.

Perceiving instantly that resistance would be futile, he said quickly and without pause, "There are people at the zoo. The security guard, acting on your father's orders, rang about ten minutes ago with the news that a section of the back fence had been torn through and a group of men in a large truck had entered the zoo grounds. It seems that they are attempting to load the animals onto the truck. I think they must be game smugglers. They must have caught wind of some of the press that's out there about our zoo. I don't know how else they would have known to come here. They would have assumed – and correctly, I might add – that our security was relatively light in comparison to other zoos that house an equally diverse population of species. It would be a lucrative haul to make off with so many animals. How many species did your father say again? Three hundred and fifty? That's an easy mark to have all of that potential merchandise huddled in one spot and relatively unguarded. We should have known that we were vulnerable."

Ginny listened in horror as Blake poured forth his almost clairvoyant rundown of the ongoing crisis at the zoo and, when at last he had seemed to finish and drew a large breath to replenish that which he had exhausted during his speech, she replied calmly, "And what did he want with you?"

She could tell that, for whatever reason, Blake had not expected her to ask this question, but, deciding fiercely against relenting, she fixed him with a look that said in no uncertain terms that an answer was compulsory.

Blake, knowing that to lie would be fruitless, went on with sincerity. "He would like for me to meet him down at the zoo so that we can decide how best to handle the situation. He does not want to involve the police. If the intruders know that we are coming it could result in them taking flight and since they already have some of the animals loaded onto their truck, we can't risk that happening. Not only would we risk them getting away, but it could potentially cause injury or death to the animals were some ill-conceived police chase to meet a fiery end."

Ginny, who had been listening with rapt attention, gave a purposeful nod that conveyed her full understanding of the situation at hand and, taking the shoes and clothing that Blake had brought forth from the other room prior to being handed the phone, she began to ready herself.

Blake, noticing this and resolving to put an immediate stop to it, took her by the hand and said, "And where do you think you're going?"

"I'm going with you," she answered dismissively.

"Your father did not wish for you to come with me. We do not fully know what is happening yet," replied Blake in alarm.

Ginny turned to face him with an expression that conveyed without the slightest room for misinterpretation, that she would be joining him and there was simply nothing that could be done to stop her.

Recognising defeat in the stubborn girl's eyes but still resolving firmly to keep her out of harm's way, Blake said, "Very well. But you have to promise to do as we say. Your father and me. If we need you to stay behind while we go inside, I need your word that you will not attempt to follow us."

Blake held her gaze, obviously awaiting a reply in the affirmative prior to bestowing his final consent.

Ginny, rolling her eyes in the manner with which those who knew her were all so familiar, said half-heartedly, "Alright, I promise. Let's go."

Blake held her gaze a little longer, as if to emphasise the seriousness of her promise and his own expectation that she not break it, then turned towards the door and exited through it, with Ginny following closely behind him.

He knew that his quickest route to the zoo would have been via his own two feet, but with Ginny unexpectedly accompanying him, and being unable to carry her for fear of revealing that which he most desired not to about himself, he led her instead to her car. He had no car of his own and reasoned that this option was the best available alternative to his own innate swiftness. The car itself was relatively unused since Ginny usually preferred to walk. As a result, they found it filthy and entrenched up to the hubcaps in some unidentifiable organic detritus that had accumulated over the many weeks since it had last moved from its spot. Despite its ramshackle outward appearance, however, the engine was true and started up immediately as soon as Blake had commanded it to do so with the turn of its key. The pair hopped in, Blake at the wheel and Ginny riding shotgun, and accelerated quickly in the direction of the accursed zoo.

When they were still about a quarter of a mile away from the main entrance, they saw a silhouetted figure standing in the road, obstructing their progress and apparently trying to wave them down. As they neared the spot where the figure stood, they realised that it was Ginny's father. The two exchanged a questioning glance and then Blake, following the commands inherent in the motion of the old man's gesturing arms, pulled the vehicle off the road and into a tree-lined alcove that lay just beyond and out of sight. When the engine had been cut and Blake and Ginny had both emerged from the car, the old man approached, looking all at once angry, surprised, and excited.

He went first to Blake and said in a harsh tone, "I thought I told you to come alone! Ginny was not to be a part of this!"

Blake looked back at him sympathetically and replied in a resigned voice that explained more than did his words the truth behind Ginny's presence, "Surely you know that your daughter won't be left behind. She refused to stay at home and it should come as no surprise that I was not able to compel her to do so. That is all there is to it. She has given me her word, however, that she will do as we say while she is here."

The old man's face dropped a little as the understanding of his daughter's strong character washed over it, and he said simply, "Very well."

With this, he left Blake and approached his beloved daughter. Looking into her eyes with a trace of sadness in his own, he said, "Why did you come?"

"You know I had to," she replied, noticing the fleeting emotion in her father's countenance and wondering as to its origin.

"If you had not, then I suppose you would not be my Ginny Harrison," said the old man sweetly, smiling slightly as he backed away from her so he could face both of the new arrivals.

Speaking in an elevated voice so that they both would be able to hear him clearly, the old man began. "I'm sorry if I worried you out on the road. I thought Mr Blake would be coming alone and so was not expecting a vehicle…" With this bizarre admission, the old man stopped himself abruptly, apparently struggling to account for the strangeness of this comment. When he could find no way to do so, he went on. "Uh, well, anyway. Fortunately, I recognised Ginny's car just in time to make myself seen on the road before you drove any further."

The old man paused to clear his throat and then turned, indicating the direction of the zoo before continuing, "There are four men inside the zoo at this very moment who seek to take our animals and sell them into what will undoubtedly be a horrible fate, if not into death itself. Not only do we have a responsibility to our animals to see that this does not happen, but we also have a responsibility to this town, this zoo, and to all of the people who have worked so long and so hard so that we could make it this far."

The old man again approached his daughter and took her hands. "Ginny, you must stay here with the car, no matter how long we take. You must promise me."

The pleading was so strong and so sincere in her father's expression that Ginny felt all of the fight drain out of her. She consented to staying with the vehicle, unable to bear the thought of causing her father any pain.

With her promise secured, the old man turned to Blake and said, "I ask you, Mr Blake, to join me in entering the zoo and attempting to thwart these criminals. I have asked our normal security detail to vacate so that we will be quite alone once we enter the premises." In response to a questioning look from Blake, he added, "The authorities lack the stealth and tact that will be necessary in order to liberate our stolen cargo without visiting any harm on those creatures that we have sworn to protect."

As he finished, he gave Blake a small wink that was oddly out of keeping with the overall tone of his speech, downplaying in secret the danger that he sought to amplify in front of his daughter. What would not be dangerous to two beings like himself and Blake, after all, would be all the more so for someone in possession of Ginny's delicate and uncorrupted human frame.

Before setting out towards the zoo, Blake turned one last time to face Ginny in order to reassure her as to his own safety in the task at hand. Without a doubt the young girl, wholly unaware as she was to the enormous preternatural advantage that both her father and Blake possessed over those with whom they were about to quarrel, was sick with worry. These were, understandably, two men that she loved more than life itself. And though neither man harboured any doubt as to his own well-being, both having challenged and easily overcome all who had sought to oppress them throughout their respective histories, the theatrics they employed in an effort to paint a picture of danger in front of Ginny, so as to keep her from encountering any in reality, had had their desired effect.

"We need to go now, Ginny," said Blake reassuringly.

Ginny, looking now as though anger were making its way slowly to the surface of her face in order to supplant the worry that had been its dominant emotion previously, answered, "This is madness, Ainsley. Why do you guys have to go when we can just call the police? This is ridiculous and I couldn't bear it if one of you were to get injured, or worse, killed. Oh, I can't even bear to think about it! Say you won't go!"

The girl collapsed into rolling sobs, but Blake remained resolute, replying calmly and simply, "I must, but you needn't worry. We will not be long and, if we are successful, which I suspect we shall be, we will have saved all that we have spent so long working towards."

Ginny looked up at him with moist eyes. She did not understand this project that her father and her lover had sought to undertake together in so unorthodox a manner, but she understood completely that she was powerless to stop them. With a final embrace of each man, she stepped back, saying nothing but indicating through the slightly stooped and submissive attitude in which she stood that they were free now to proceed as they wished. A few seconds later, they were gone, disappeared into the dark trees that surrounded the endangered zoo which was to be their battlefield.

The two men entered the tree line slowly at first, then, when they were certain that Ginny could no longer see them, employed the full power of their unnatural speed and were at the zoo's perimeter fence within seconds. The lofty fence was twelve feet high but, being long familiar with the immense strength unique to their kind, they knew that placing themselves on the other side of it would be no great challenge. Instead of hopping the great fence, however, and running the risk of revealing their presence prematurely, the two men began to investigate along its out-facing wall in hopes of first establishing the entry point of the uninvited guests. Perhaps they might even discover their present location within the grounds and gain an even greater edge. Blake and the old man each knew that, despite their near invulnerability, it was not wise to enter into a potentially dangerous environment without first having completed at least some level of reconnaissance.

The two men continued moving swiftly along the fence line until, after a few minutes, the determined vigilantes discovered a set of parallel tire tracks that diverged from an old and overgrown country road that snaked through the lofty trees, almost entirely forgotten in time by the whole of the town.

They followed the tracks without difficulty through a mess of bent metal and splintered wood that had once been a large section of the zoo's back fence, clearly where the perpetrators had entered. The deeply entrenched earth gave evidence of the sturdy wall's loyal resistance but in the end, it had succumbed to the overwhelming force of the truck and fallen. It appeared, however, that the intruders had not been entirely confident in the truck's ability to get the job done because, just off from the tire tracks, Blake noticed a small pallet that had been offloaded. Stacked on top were what must have been at least twenty or thirty pale-coloured, chalky bricks, each labelled: *TANNERITE (1lb)*.

Blake and the old man speculated that these crude explosives were likely brought as a backup measure in the event that the raw horsepower and immense weight of the enormous truck were to prove insufficient in felling the heavy wall and something more powerful was needed, even if it was a less desirous option given the noise that would have necessarily accompanied any concussive explosion. As to the type of explosive employed, they could only guess that so rudimentary a combustible had been selected due simply to its commercial availability as well as the ease with which it could be detonated.

The two men, both making an effort to remain hidden and taking care to give the large pile of explosives a wide berth, peeked their heads through one of the missing fence sections and scanned for signs of life. It did not take them long to spot those whom they sought. There was a large truck, not quite a semi but more than a U-Haul, parked and idling next to one of the zoo's large enclosures with a trailer attached that was clearly retrofitted for animal transport.

Leaning unguarded against one of the truck's back tires were several rifles of unknown calibre, belonging to unseen owners. They watched, and after a few minutes one of the culprits emerged from the shadows wheeling a dolly on which a large crate stood with air holes drilled into it. Once he had offloaded his cargo onto the trailer, he returned to the shadows. This exchange went on for a while, featuring different individuals pushing or pulling various-sized crates and offloading them in turn. They had counted three men in total, including two of such abnormally large stature that both Blake and the old man concluded instantly that they were the same as those they had seen entering Proust earlier that afternoon.

The old man turned to Blake with a concerned expression and whispered, "Aren't there supposed to be four of them?"

Blake shrugged his shoulders and replied, "You told me four, but that is all I know."

The old man seemed to be thinking fast. Out next to the truck, the three men had congregated together and seemed to be taking a momentary break from their criminal enterprise in order to rest their tired muscles. Even for the two giants, moving animals that did not want to be moved was no easy task.

Noticing that the three men had all come together as easy prey in a single place and within their lines of sight, the old man, discarding his suspicion of a fourth perpetrator so as not to miss this opportunity of bringing the ordeal to a swift and easy close, said to Blake, "Let's get them. Now. Move in!"

Producing a long cord from a small satchel that hung around his neck, the old man burst forth from the breach in the fence and rushed towards the unsuspecting thieves. Blake, taking the briefest of moments to process the abrupt change in plan, dug his heels into the soft earth and found himself at the old man's side almost instantly. As they neared the still unaware criminals, Blake took one end of the cord and sped ahead. He encircled the three men with the cord and was back around to Ginny's father again before the old man had even reached the group.

By the time the three intruders even realised that a cord had somehow appeared out of thin air, wrapped itself around them and was quickly forcing them all together, Blake had already made five complete revolutions around them, dashing any hope of escape. To the three bound men it did not seem to be the work of men but rather looked as though a dark cloud had descended upon them. Through the fog they could barely perceive a black-headed figure that they all believed must be a demon staring back at them. The cord duplicated its coils as if by magic and bound them together across their chests and legs, tightening and drawing them closer as it multiplied without any apparent source, save the demon that stood just beyond the dark veil. The horrible face staring in at them through the gloom and blur seemed to be smiling in triumph, and they recoiled in terror at this divine reckoning that sought to punish their many sins at last.

When the black cloud subsided and the bound men finally opened the eyes that they had shut tight in terror, they saw that their conquerors were but two men, seemingly of flesh and blood. There was the demon, which had terrified them throughout their ordeal, looking very much of human origin now that the confusion and panic brought on by the dark cloud had lifted, and then another, whom before now had remained unseen.

The demon approached the other and said, "You are quite fast, Mr Blake. Well done."

The compliment produced no effect on the one called Blake, who busied himself securing the cord so that it would not lose its tautness. Within the coils, one of the two giants seemed to have fainted due to fright and remained unconscious while the other sobbed uncontrollably, apparently unable to regain mastery of his own faculties in the wake of this unprecedented shock. Both would have sworn without a doubt that they had been reproached by the Devil himself. The third bound man, however, did not cry, nor did he faint. Instead, he narrowed his eyes suspiciously and studied the two men in a calculating fashion.

"How was it that you did what you did?" Rand Patrick asked of his captors.

The two men, however, ignored him as they deliberated with one another just out of earshot.

When the voluminous tears of the colossus at his side began to wet Rand's right shoulder, his attention was brought back to his afflicted comrades. He looked up with disgust and yelled, "Get it together, man!"

He attempted to elbow the bulging abdomen of the retching leviathan, which was the only part of the enormous body that resided within reach of Rand's elbow, but found that he could not move due to the skilfully applied cords that held him. Turning his attention away from the comically large, heaving figure pressed to his side, he glanced back again at the two men who were still conversing softly, still beyond the range of his hearing. Rand had never seen anything like what had just happened. What had just happened was not possible and yet, here they were.

As Rand Patrick was considering the impossibility of his current predicament, Ainsley Blake and Ginny's father discussed seriously what was to become of the captured men.

"Now that we have secured the safety of our animals, it will be safe to call the proper authorities and let them take over from here," said the old man to Blake.

Blake considered this for a while, his brow furled, then replied, "I suppose you're right. The story that they will tell will not be believed. The darkness can play tricks on the eyes, that much is well known."

The old man went on. "We must ask them not to inform the press. I can see no reason to postpone tomorrow's event, and the knowledge of tonight's break-in may make people uncomfortable were they to find out. These things have a way of becoming exaggerated as they travel through the unreliable filter of the mob and I'd prefer not to risk it."

Blake nodded in agreement and asked, "And what about the back fence?"

Ginny's father thought for a moment and then answered, "We can rope the area off, put up some temporary fencing and inform the public that that section of the back fence has not yet been fully completed. Renovations always take longer than promised."

With their course of action thus decided, the two men turned back to their captives and approached them. Of the three men, only one seemed to be in his right mind. One of the two giants was slumped and motionless, held up only by the cord that bound him, while the other was wailing like a giant baby. The third, normal-sized man, however, was staring fixedly at his two captors as if trying to discover their secret, completely devoid of any discernible fear. The man's calmness unnerved Blake, but, trusting in the strength of the cord that secured him and in the integrity of his own knot that held it in place, he quickly dismissed his concern.

"Gentlemen," announced the old man to the group of bound trespassers at large. "We will be notifying the police of what has transpired here tonight and releasing you into their custody. Mr Blake, if you would please make the call. There is a phone at the concession stand just over there."

The old man indicated one of the stands closest to them and Blake made to comply. He had made only a few steps in the direction of the phone when a voice called out from somewhere unseen.

"Not so fast there, mate."

A man, in his late thirties or early forties, Blake couldn't tell which, emerged from the shadows. The fourth man, whom they had so imprudently dismissed, approached them now. To the horror of the two almost-conquerors, he was not alone. Walking directly in front of him, and acting as a shield between himself and the two men who had so effortlessly triumphed over his henchmen, was a terrified and white-faced Ginny. The girl's father let slip a wail that spoke for both him and Blake as he stared in shock at his beloved daughter.

"There you are, Bruce," said Rand Patrick slyly from within his bindings. "I was wondering where you'd gone off to!"

The appearance of their missing comrade seemed to have a positive effect on the incapacitated group of thieves. The large one, who had been in the midst of a deep swoon ever since the appearance of Blake and the old man, finally reopened his eyes and looked around confusedly, as though dazed. His equally large counterpart, however, continued howling into the night, apparently still lost in the terror that his supernatural encounter had inspired within him. Rand, calm even prior to Bruce's arrival, looked positively jubilant and hunger shone in his beady eyes.

Bruce did not look at Rand when he spoke, but instead stared unblinkingly at Blake and the old man, determined not to give them any opportunity of regaining the upper hand.

Blake and the old man, both perceiving at once the pistol that was placed at the back of Ginny's head, did not dare make a move. Indeed, it was true that they were in possession of a speed that might allow them to gain control of their attacker's weapon prior to him having had a chance to discharge it, but it was not a risk that either was willing to take. It was also true that by using the unique gifts with which they were endowed, they would be revealing their true natures to the one person for whom they had worked so diligently in order that she might be spared the burden of their curse.

Therefore, it was decided between the two men, without speaking a word to each other, that they had no choice but to comply with this Bruce's demands for the time being and when the time came to mount their offensive, they would fight as would ordinary men.

"I'm going to need you to untie my boys," said Bruce, matter-of-factly, not daring to lower his eyes from the two men, nor the pistol from the back of Ginny's head.

Blake and the old man exchanged a glance that reconfirmed the course of action that each had committed to on his own: that the advantages on which they had counted up to this point would no longer be of service to them now that Ginny was present. They moved slowly to the encircled men and made to untie them. The sobbing giant screamed louder than ever as the two men, whom he still believed to be minions of the devil and there to claim his soul, approached in the darkness. In a few seconds the coils had loosened and, shortly thereafter, the cord fell limply to the ground, freeing Bruce Kelly's three compatriots from their bondage.

"That's good," said Bruce. "Now back away from them and stand over there."

Bruce indicated an area away from both the freed men and their weapons, which remained leaning at the rear of the truck. Blake and the old man complied.

Bruce, seeing that his orders were followed, went on. "Alright, you two just stay right there and don't move. Rand, you keep loading the merchandise. And Dougie, will you get your worthless friend under control? I can't stand to hear that bloody wailing."

The enormous Dougie, still recovering from his faint, turned to his hysterical counterpart and attempted to console him while Rand busied himself loading more crates.

Blake and the old man sat where they had been told and took in the spectacle, neither clear as to what should be done next. They watched as the giant called Dougie tried in vain to silence the cries of his equally large companion who, despite his friend's efforts, remained stubbornly inconsolable. They watched the one now loading crates called Rand, who had remained unconcerned throughout his captivity because he had known that a fourth member of their team had been forgotten, and so retained his liberty, and would surely be coming for them. Finally, they watched Bruce, the clear leader of them all, who oversaw the whole operation.

He had not moved to assist his men in any way and instead remained as he had been with his pistol pressed to the back of Ginny's head, his eyes darting from the two immense nitwits engaged in their absurd spectacle, to the third man loading crates, and then to his two prisoners and back again. He dared not lower the pistol, for he knew that the two men who were held captive by it had, prior to his arrival on the scene, easily overcome his three henchmen when they had been given the opportunity to do so, and he was determined that they not have it a second time.

After what seemed like an eternity to the two hostages, the work of loading crates seemed to be tapering off. When the one called Rand emerged from the trailer wheeling an empty dolly and announcing that the truck was full, they both knew that their time had run out. Still unsure as to what could be done, they did not move. Bruce, in response to Rand's announcement, turned to address them, Ginny still at his front and held fast by the threat of the pistol at the back of her head.

The two men listened intently as he began to speak. "Gentlemen, I'm sure that you can understand that I cannot permit you to go free. You have seen me and you have seen my men. It's nothing personal, as they say."

Ginny's father looked at Blake in alarm, speechless and knowing that the time to act was now, but still not knowing how. Blake thought hard, racking his wise brain for a course of action that continued to elude him. All he could think was that they were finished if something were not done.

There was no alternative; it was time to take the risk. Time to reveal his true nature to the one he loved and accept the consequences of doing so. If it meant that he had to lose her then so be it. She would fear him, disown him, perhaps, but at least she would be alive to make the choice, instead of dead with her love intact. Blake made to rise and charge his oppressor when, suddenly, he saw a silhouetted figure dart out from the shadows and within the blink of an eye, the pistol was removed from Bruce's hand and his body thrown sideways with such force that he travelled airborne for several yards before landing hard and crumpling onto the ground. Ginny was freed and safe for now. She stood still for some time, unsure as to the source of her liberation, when a short, rounded man appeared as if from thin air behind her, smiling jovially at the shocked group.

"Hugo!" cried Blake, rushing forward to meet his friend. "You've saved us! I can't believe you are here. Oh, welcome back, Hugo! Welcome back!"

Hugo continued smiling at Blake's ecstatic face and answered, "Seems I got here just in time, my dear friend."

"How did you know?" asked Blake in utter disbelief.

"I returned to town to find you, Blake, and was passing some time at the coffee shop that young Ginny here is so fond of when I overheard these men discussing their despicable plan over coffee. I resolved then and there that I would be present on the scene when their crime was to take place so that I might be able to stop it, and perhaps by doing so make amends for my abrupt departure from you so long ago."

Blake nodded, smiling, and said, "There are no amends to be made, my friend, but thank you, Hugo."

Rand Patrick, witnessing that the scales had once again tipped in favour of the opposition, retreated into the darkness of the trailer so as to remain unseen. Bruce, knocked momentarily unconscious by the severity of the good doctor's blow, began to stir just as the two reconciled friends were wrapping up their conversation and by the time Blake was offering his final thanks to his returned friend, he was again fully awake.

Blake, noticing that Bruce was rising to his feet, turned quickly to Hugo and whispered, "Ginny does not know what we are. Therefore, we fight tonight as men. Nothing more."

Hugo gave a nod that conveyed his full understanding of the situation, betraying only a hint of disappointment at not being permitted to employ his full potential. They both turned to face Bruce, as did Ginny and her father.

Bruce, apparently wishing to avoid taking on the four capable adults all by himself, called to his comrades, "Rand, get your ass out here. This isn't finished yet!"

As Rand reluctantly emerged from the dark interior of the trailer to rejoin the fray, Bruce turned his gaze to the two loafing behemoths who had been so preoccupied up to this point that they were still wholly unaware of Hugo's arrival on the scene, or the subsequent disarmament of their leader. One remained still lost in the immutable sobs that overpowered his reason and carried away his reality, while the other dutifully, albeit unsuccessfully, attempted to restore his calm.

A look of supreme annoyance flashed across Bruce's face with the realisation that he was a man down, and he yelled, "Dammit, Dougie! Leave Mike there and get over here!"

Dougie looked down one more time at the pathetic, heaving Mike, then left him there to join his other companions.

The two groups faced each other. Blake, Hugo, Ginny and her father on one side. Bruce, Rand and the towering Dougie on the other.

It was Ginny's father who spoke first. "Gentlemen, you have failed. Leave this place now, without the animals, and no harm will come to you."

It was Rand who spoke for the other side. "I don't think so. We came a long way for this and we're not leaving without our haul. You should never have come down here to stop us. The girl's blood will be on your hands."

When he finished speaking, Rand exchanged a look with Bruce and Blake thought that he perceived a slight conspiratorial smile pass between the two men.

Before Blake could be sure of what he had seen, however, Rand yelled, "Now!"

Turning away from the battle, Rand and Bruce both broke away from the group and ran back in the direction of the trailer from which Rand had just emerged. Blake knew instantly that they were going for the guns and acted in accordance with his first impulse.

Turning to Ginny with panic written across his features, he screamed, "Ginny! Run! Run now!"

Ginny, unaware as to her own danger but not daring to question Blake's command, turned on her heels and ran for the breach in the zoo's back gate as fast as her legs would carry her. She had almost reached the opening when Bruce and Rand arrived at their weapons. Rand directed his aim at the three men while Bruce, bent solely on revenge for the attempted thwarting of his criminal enterprise, took aim at the fleeing girl. He squeezed the trigger with too much haste, however, and sent his first few rounds into the earth at her feet. Ginny, correctly assuming that the sounds she heard following her were bullets, dove for cover behind a pile of debris just within the fence's opening that had been fortuitously deposited there when the large truck had initially made its entrance into the zoo.

Bruce continued to oppress her with fire while Rand, aiming in the opposite direction, attempted to rid them of the three male components of the opposition. The three men, in order to prevent Rand from having a good shot, all separated, forcing the shooter to engage them individually rather than en masse, and began to close in on him, zigging and zagging as they neared the increasingly flustered shooter. With Ginny hidden out of sight behind the downed section of fence, the three men were now free to employ their supernatural speed and within seconds, they had overpowered Rand and relieved him of his weapon.

With Rand incapacitated, Hugo turned his attention to the giant Dougie who, despite his enormous size, remained no match for the preternatural strength of an unrestrained Hugo Wegener. As Hugo was easily overcoming his opponent without any need of assistance, Blake and the old man, both moved by the same force, turned their attention immediately to Ginny. She was still hiding behind the pile of downed fence while Bruce continued peppering the entire section with gunfire, keeping the young girl pinned. Blake began to start towards Bruce until he noticed something with horror.

Turning white-faced back to Ginny's father, he yelled, "The Tannerite! He's going to hit the Tannerite!"

The old man turned his gaze back to his daughter and noticed with dread that the small pallet of crude explosive was indeed in dangerously close proximity to the spot his daughter had chosen for her refuge. It was only by some miracle that it had remained so far unscathed by the gunfire that continued to splash all around it. Moved by that paternal instinct common to all fathers of the earth, he shot out in the direction of his daughter like a rocket, utilising every ounce of speed available to him.

He reached her just as the fateful bullet met with the small pallet of explosives and, grabbing his daughter and turning his back towards the igniting pallet so that he would absorb the bulk of the explosive energy himself, he hurled her out of harm's way and free of the blast radius. As Ginny flew away from the epicentre of the blooming explosion, seemingly in slow motion, she looked back to her father and watched with horror as he was engulfed entirely in flames. She screamed for him, convinced as she was that she would never again see his face, until the shockwave of the explosion rocketed him out of the fireball with the force of a freight train, sending him tumbling through the air to land with force amongst the mass of twisted metal and broken wood that comprised the felled section of the back fence.

For a while all was quiet. Bruce had apparently been knocked unconscious again due to his own close proximity to the blast, while Blake and Ginny both looked on in shock, terrified at what they might find once the smoke cleared. When the dust finally settled, they saw the old man. He lay on the ground, motionless, his eyes wide and staring straight up into the sky at something invisible to the rest of the living world. Harpooned through his chest was a bloodstained piece of jagged wood, forced through the entire width of his body by the immense force of the blast, a splintered and broken relic of the once-great protecting wall that surrounded the ill-fated zoo.

Ginny ran immediately to him and kneeled at his side. Blake joined her but remained standing. The old man still lived, though he seemed far away. Behind them, Bruce once again began to stir, but it was of no consequence. Hugo had finished nicely with the brutish Dougie and had even secured the whimpering Mike as a precautionary measure, though he believed him to be of no real threat to them in his present state. Now the good doctor stood sentinel over the defeated Bruce while the others tended to the old man.

"I'm so sorry, Daddy," Ginny said, burying her face in her father's shoulder. "This is all my fault. I tried to stay by the car, but I had to see what you guys were doing. I was so worried; I just couldn't stay there not knowing. Oh, Daddy. I'm so sorry."

The old man seemed to return again to the realm of the living in response to his daughter's voice and even managed a slight smile as he said weakly, "You have nothing to be sorry about, sweetheart. I have lived more fortunately than have most men, because I have loved so deeply. You. Your mother. You both gave me that love and, with it, my life meaning. One could live a thousand lives without ever having found it." He shot Blake a surreptitious look that said indeed he almost had, and then turned back to his daughter, saying with both gentleness and finality, "I am a lucky man." The fading old man then turned his attention fully to Blake and went on quietly. "Ainsley. Come here."

Blake kneeled down low to the man's face so that he could hear the voice that was growing softer with each passing moment.

When he was in position, the old man continued, "She is yours now. Remember everything we discussed. You said once that I had taught you much. I implore you now to remember those lessons."

Blake nodded, his eyes betraying his wrenching heart, and said, "I will. Always."

The old man appeared satisfied and turned once more to his daughter. "You are the love of my life, Virginia Harrison."

With that said, the old man turned his hollowing gaze back to his invisible angels in the sky. Ginny watched the face that had always been so youthful, despite its age, now tired-looking, pale and lined. She watched as the resolve to live drained from him and his stare grew more and more vacant. And finally, she watched as he let go his final exhale, setting free the life that had been granted to him in order that it might return from whence it came and give rise to those future generations whose turn on Earth was still to come. The great man's eyes closed and he was gone forever.

Ginny, trembling as she searched her father's still face for signs of life, sank into deep sobs, screaming, "Oh, Daddy! I'm so sorry. Oh, no! Oh, no!"

The orphaned girl lay down next to her father's marble figure and buried her face in his shoulder, letting her tears fall in torrents. They were the tears of a broken-hearted daughter who would miss the father she loved. They were the tears of one who has lost the very last of one's family and is now all that remains of a once-proud line. And finally, they were the tears of a young girl, vulnerable, as we humans all are, to that force called love and the unbearable sadness that follows in the wake of its loss, and she poured them forth without shame.

After a few minutes spent bearing witness to Ginny's misery, Blake rose from his spot at the old man's side and turned his attention back to Bruce, who still remained the captive of the good Doctor Wegener. The moment Bruce perceived the frenzied rage that flashed in Blake's eyes, he panicked and attempted to take flight.

With Ginny wholly absorbed in her mourning, Blake had no need of holding back and was upon the murderer in an instant, his preternatural glow radiating out of him in all directions and terrifying his less evolved adversary. He flipped the desperately flailing Bruce onto his back and dug his strong fingers into the man's soft throat without mercy or hesitation. Bruce's eyes widened with fear as he felt the pressure on his trachea increase with each passing second. All he could see were the wild eyes of Ainsley Blake staring back into his own and glowing red with fury.

Bruce recognised in those fiery eyes the same anger, hurt and savagery that had been present in each of the countless beasts of the African continent that had fallen before his infamous rifle. Each of them surfaced in his recollection now and joined within the form of Ainsley Blake to exact their revenge on the man who had deprived them of their own right to life.

Bruce tasted the blood that was beginning to pool in the back of his throat and with a painful cough that forced its way through his constricted airways, he saw the spray of red liquid speckle the fierce and inhuman features of Ainsley Blake. His world began to spin and darken as the horrible spectres of butchered animals danced around him, digging their feet into the ground and roaring in triumph as if performing some macabre tribal dance in his honour.

He had always known that some great beast would come for him, and that beast had found its form within a man who had been called by a thousand names, and who had lived a thousand lives. There was no humanity in this man. There was only the insanity of revenge and the ferocity of the beast. Bruce's final thought, before the darkness overcame him, was that this was a fitting end, and so, with something almost akin to peace, he gave himself freely over to death and struggled no more.

As soon as it became apparent that Bruce had begun to fade from life, Blake knew that it was time to end it. And so, with one final and irreversible act, the savage culmination of his supreme vengeance, Blake plunged his talon-like fingers straight through the delicate skin of Bruce's neck, penetrating deep into the warm blood that flowed just beneath the surface and savouring his kill as would a lion.

He wanted it and now that he had achieved it, he basked in it. He looked down at the murderous face and watched as it changed gradually from panicked to peaceful. He kept watching as the rosy colour of the flushed cheeks drained out and then appeared again, this time as a dark pool that was spreading just underneath Bruce's motionless head. He felt the pulsing current of warm blood cease its life-giving movement beneath the skin of the punctured neck, and with this small but powerful affirmation of his crime, his humanity, lost temporarily to the madness of his vengeance, began slowly to trickle back to him.

Blake looked up from his silent victim with tears in his eyes. The good doctor stood over him, looking serious and saddened.

Ginny still remained crying over her father's body, oblivious to all else. The three surviving members of Bruce's gang sat without moving or speaking, bound once more by the same cord from which they had been liberated no more than an hour previously. The two hulking leviathans were both crying now, but each for different reasons. The sly smile had long since vanished from Rand Patrick's solemn face.

Blake inhaled deeply, and with the restorative air filling his lungs, he felt his remaining humanity, which he had abandoned so many years ago, return to him in its full glory at last. It was pain, and it was love, the one being both the cause and cure of the other. It was gratitude, friendship and feeling. It was life, in short, the only kind of life that could ever be worth living. To breathe without it is not to live, but to be less than dead.

Blake looked over at Ginny and, after nodding appreciatively to Hugo one last time, he went to her.

As he held his weeping love, he glanced around at the cages and thought about what the old man had told him. It was over for him now. In this place, full of all manner of God's beasts, he could lock away forever that part of himself that was also beast.

To be kept safely among its brethren. To protect the people who would always be threatened by it, so long as it were allowed to exist unrestrained. To protect Ginny and to protect himself too. Blake knew they would open the zoo on the next day because it had been the dream of the old man whom they both had loved so much. It was for him that they would persevere now in the wake of such great loss. It was for him that they would hold on to this place and to each other. He had sacrificed himself so that his beloved daughter could live, and Blake knew that she would sooner die herself than allow his sacrifice to have been in vain.

-PART FOUR-

- I -

THE REST OF THE NIGHT FOLLOWING THE ROBBERY WOULD remain forever a blur in the mind of Virginia Harrison. She had not, after all, borne witness to a great deal of the events as they had actually transpired, at least, not with enough clarity to have any legitimate idea of their reality. She had spent a portion of the night trapped behind a pile of fence debris, desperately avoiding gunfire, and the other portion crying into the shoulder of her dead father. She had not seen her lover's merciless act of vengeance, nor had she noticed the supernatural abilities of his portly friend, whom prior to that she had never met. She didn't care, though. She only knew that the battle was over and that her side had been victorious, if you could call it that given what it had cost them. She also knew that she was tired and out of tears.

The police had come, and an ambulance. Not because they had been called, but because explosions and gunfire in a small town are more than enough to rouse the collective suspicion of one's neighbours. Within a few minutes of the battle's commencement, the station had received calls from just about every single household within a ten-mile radius. The police had arrived on the scene to find Blake and Ginny kneeling over the old man, and Hugo standing guard over their prisoners. The weight of despair had been so great, and so tangible to those who had arrived later on the scene, that any scolding from the authorities, which might otherwise have been justified in response to the vigilantism of the zoo owners, was discarded in favour of a more sympathetic approach.

Blankets and hot coffee were provided to Ginny, who sat on the back fender of a parked ambulance being comforted by a plump, soft-spoken and motherly female officer, who very much looked the part she was there to play. Blake and Hugo stood in conversation with several male officers, rehashing the events of the night. The three living intruders were loaded into the back of a squad van, where they were to be transferred to the local holding cell until morning when they could be processed and sent on to county. As for their deceased leader, his cause of death was determined to be an animal attack. This had not been some fiction created by Blake or Hugo but by one of the officers who had been the first to begin taking their statements. Noticing the deep puncture wounds on Bruce Kelly's ravaged neck, and seeing the animals loaded haphazardly into crates that looked to him dangerously flimsy in their construction, the young officer had formed his own theory as to the probable cause of death and, when he presented it to Blake and Hugo without first asking them for their version of the truth, they had simply decided not to correct the assumptions he had made.

When the police had finally wrapped up their onsite investigation, there not being much to do since the guilty party had already been apprehended, and the official vehicles began to pull away, Blake looked for Ginny. He found her again at her father's side, bidding him a final farewell as the morgue officials waited patiently and respectfully to take the corpse.

Once he was loaded, Blake spoke to Ginny. "You go with them. I will come for you soon. Hugo and I will stay and take care of things here."

Ginny did not say anything but moved her blanketed self into him so that he could embrace her. When she pulled away, she gave him an appreciative nod, her eyes puffy and glistening in the moonlight, and then got into the front seat of the hearse that had been summoned for the occasion once all hope of saving the old man had been abandoned by the responding EMTs. Blake and Hugo watched as the last vehicles exited the zoo.

-II-

THE FOLLOWING MORNING, BLAKE WAS AT GINNY'S apartment. After a long night spent alternately between the morgue and the police station, the young girl had been on the verge of collapse when Blake had finally arrived and taken charge of her. She hadn't wanted to leave her father's body, but once Blake arrived and assured her that there wasn't anything more that could be done that night, she gave in to her exhaustion at last and allowed herself to be taken home.

She had slept only an hour or so when Blake roused her again and told her that there was some place they needed to be. Ginny, having forgotten everything leading up to her father's death and, moreover, not thinking clearly due to sleep deprivation, had no idea where they could possibly be going in such a time as this. She was so tired, however, and so glazed over that she lacked the strength to argue and so obliged his request without any protest. She rose without a single word in the way of acknowledgement and went to the washroom to freshen herself up. Blake listened for a bit until he heard the water running and then, satisfied that she would be returning shortly and ready to go, made himself comfortable on her couch.

Fifteen minutes later, Ginny emerged from the bathroom, hair dripping and devoid of makeup but still looking more refreshed than she had going in. Blake rose from his seat and went to her. She still did not speak but put her head on his shoulder to let him know that she appreciated that he was there. They stood silently for a few long and peaceful moments.

The warmth of the embrace seemed to fortify her and she finally said in a soft voice, "Okay, let's go then, I guess."

Blake separated from her and gazed down into her sad eyes. There was something enormously tragic in witnessing a spirit that had been so full of happiness and laughter be stripped of its light in the wake of a great human act of evil. He considered to himself that, to take something pure and unscathed and force something dark through it, leaving a permanent stain and tarnishing forever its uncorrupted shine, was a thing profoundly immoral. A sin without the possibility of forgiveness. He fought back tears as he peered into those eyes, searching them desperately for any sign that they might have retained at least some hint of their former brightness.

It crushed him to find nothing within them, but he held back his lamentations and, composing himself, said with forced serenity, "Let's go. There is something you need to see."

The pair exited the building in silence and went to Ginny's car. She assumed Blake must have driven it back from where it had been left the night before and so did not ask any questions. He opened the passenger side door for her and then closed it softly once she had seated herself. Walking swiftly around the front of the car, he seated himself behind the wheel.

They drove in silence and reached the town's main street within a few minutes. Ginny was so preoccupied that she did not notice that the town's main drag, usually bustling with activity around this time on weekends, was completely abandoned. Not a soul roamed the desolate stretch of sun-parched asphalt. Once they had crossed through the town, however, the traffic began to thicken.

The sudden change seemed to rouse Ginny from her reverie and she straightened up in her seat. To her utter surprise, she found the street teeming with people. It seemed that, being unable to drive any further due to the traffic jam, they had simply abandoned their cars and left them parked in the street so that they could continue on foot. Adding to this already strange spectacle was the unexplainably jovial mood of the people, exactly opposite to that which would be shared by most commuters who chanced to find themselves victims of similarly hopeless traffic conditions. In place of the anger and curse words one might expect to encounter in such a situation, there was only laughter and smiles. People were chatting happily as they walked in large groups, helping each other to carry strollers, bags and other things. There wasn't a single sad or angry face visible in the whole lot of them. After a few minutes of wide-eyed staring, Ginny realised where they were. This was the road leading to the zoo.

She looked at Blake in amazement and he smiled back at her. Popping open her door, she got to her feet, staring around at the crowd. Some of the walking folks recognised her and waved. She waved back involuntarily without thinking, looking over the top of the car again at Blake, who had vacated his seat and gotten to his feet as well. It looked like she wanted to say something but couldn't find the words. He didn't press her.

Instead, he walked around the front of the car, reversing the sombre transit he had made earlier that morning when leaving her apartment, and found her on the other side. He held out a hand to her and she took it, once again allowing herself to be led by the man she trusted. They walked through the crowd, people smiling and waving at them from all directions. A small girl, seized by a moment of mad bravery, ran up to Ginny and handed her a delicate, hand-picked flower before dissolving back into the crowd, red-faced and beaming. Ginny smiled around at everyone as they walked.

When they reached the entrance of the zoo, she saw a small group of people that included the town's mayor, as well as Blake's plump friend, Hugo, standing there as if anticipating their arrival. The huge "GRAND OPENING" ribbon that had been stored months ago in anticipation of this event had been unearthed by parties unknown and was now strung across the front gates of the entrance. The short, corpulent man called Hugo beamed at Ginny as she approached and stepped forward to greet her.

"I don't believe I have yet had the pleasure, officially." The good doctor gave her a slight bow as he spoke and extended his hand. She took it as he continued, "Of course, Mr Blake has told me so much about you that I feel as though we are already old friends. I am Dr Hugo Wegener and I am absolutely charmed to finally meet you, my dear."

He uncoiled from his bow and stepped back.

In the hand that had not participated in his introduction, he held a large pair of ceremonial novelty scissors that he now held out to her. "I believe the honour is yours, madame."

He gave another slight bow and then returned to his place in line amongst the rest of the group.

Ginny beamed around at everyone present, still unable to speak. The townspeople, still walking en masse from their stilled vehicles, now conglomerated just before the gates and stood waiting in front of the small group standing beneath the zoo's entrance. The mayor, realising that the crowd was expecting someone to say a few words and understanding that Ginny was in no condition to do so, stepped forward. He was, after all, a politician, or, as he half-jokingly and annoyingly referred to it, a "professional public speaker".

The mayor delivered his impromptu speech to the expecting crowd, touching on points like the greatness of the achievement that was the zoo, the sadness of the townspeople at the untimely death of the man who had made it all possible, the celebration of the grand opening and the subsequent unity of the whole town.

He pressed upon the point that, more than just a commercial endeavour, the zoo represented something great that had been lost to the town long ago and was now finally restored. He said that the grand opening was more than just a celebration, more than just an invitation to share in the majesty of the zoo, but also a tribute to the great man who had brought his dream to life, and whom they had only just lost. Ginny had feared that once the mayor began speaking, his words might return her to the dark place in which she had spent the morning, prior to having arrived at the zoo and finding liberation from her torment in the warm hearts of the townspeople. Listening to the praises of her late father, however, she took solace in his words instead and drew strength from them.

She looked out at the whole of the town, at her lifelong friends and at Blake. She stopped her scanning gaze when the crowd parted and Dub emerged with tears in his eyes. Ginny ran to him immediately and threw herself into his waiting arms. He held her for a long time without speaking. When they separated, he stepped back to look at her, his eyes beaming with pride as he beheld her strength, her accomplishment. She beamed back at him through tears of mingled happiness and grief. Dub had always cared for her as if she were his own, and she had done the same for him. Now, they were everything to each other; the only family left to either of them. The surrogate father and the adopted daughter, both marked by loss, and each filling the hole carved out by that loss in the other's heart.

Dub pulled Ginny back into another warm embrace and whispered paternally in her ear, "I am so proud of you, Virginia. So very proud."

They parted again and Ginny, taking the sweet man by the hand, led him away from the crowd and to Blake, who shook the old man's hand.

Dub beamed up at him and said, "I guess I owe you another 'thank you'. You seem to have a knack for saving lives around here. Let's hope it's a skill that you won't have any use for anymore, but thank you all the same, Ainsley Blake."

Blake smiled at him and gave a slight bow that conveyed his own gratitude for everything the old man had done in service to Ginny's happiness. The three of them, a family consecrated in tragedy and made blood through love, turned to face the crowd that was now cheering in the wake of the mayor's speech. In response to an invitation from the mayor, Ginny approached the ribbon and, brandishing the giant scissors for everyone to see, bisected the banner with a single snip. The crowd moved into the gates as a single entity, flowing like a storm-swelled river forcing its way through narrowed banks. Dub, Ginny and Blake stood to the side and watched them enter. When the last of them had made it through the gates, they turned and followed the crowd into the zoo.

-III-

INSIDE THE TRIUMPHANT ZOO, EVERYTHING LOOKED PERFECT.
Ginny could not understand how everything had come together
so quickly in the wake of the previous evening's tragedy. Hugo,
who had waited for them inside the gates, took it upon himself to
explain to her in his kindest manner, careful to give Blake most of
the credit, how they had toiled into the wee hours of the morning
in order to ensure that her father's dream would come to fruition
in exact accordance with what his wishes had been. He explained
how they had offloaded each of the animals that had been placed
in the trailer and returned them to their respective habitats, fed
and unharmed. How, after the police and emergency vehicles had
departed and the truck was towed off to the impound yard, they
had erected temporary fencing in order to obscure the large breach
in the back fence and keep the zoo's visitors out of harm's way.
And finally, how Blake had persuaded the local media outlets to
run a story first thing in the morning about what had happened,
or at least parts of it, and to declare absolutely that the zoo would
proceed with the opening as planned.

Noticing the effect that his words were having on Ginny, and
spurred on by the gratitude that was evident in her features, the

good doctor went on and on in the fashion typical of his good nature. He said that everything else had all just fallen into place without much effort needed on their part. The employees, after all, had come to work that morning completely unaware that anything out of the ordinary had transpired whatsoever, most of them having arrived before any news of the incident had broken.

Ginny walked the familiar zoo path and listened, flanked by Hugo on one side, who rambled on, and Dub on the other, who held her arm supportively, as though she might fall if he were to release it. Blake, as was his custom, trailed a few feet behind, playing his usual role of observer rather than participant. He watched Ginny smile but knew that there were still a great many tears left to cry. Her time to mourn still lay before her. She had not yet had time to consider and accept the enormity of her loss, and Blake understood that when the many voices that surrounded her now went silent, she would have to face it.

He thought of the elder Blake, the man whom he had chosen as his father, and the pain he had suffered in the wake of that loss. He thought of Dub, whose role in Ginny's life was hereafter to be forever changed and made more important than ever before. And he thought of Hugo, the good-natured doctor, who stood so far from tragedy even when it was right next to him, smiling through it all and infecting those around him with his own good cheer.

Hugo was a light in this time of darkness, and Blake was even more grateful for his return. When Ginny turned to look back at Blake, he saw that the fire that had so terrified him in its absence had reignited in her eye. Just a spark. A whisper of its former glory, but still it was there. The dark cloud that had obscured her light had parted and Blake knew that though the road ahead would be long and difficult, in the end her beautiful nature would prevail over her misfortune.

- IV -

A FEW WEEKS LATER, BLAKE AND GINNY WALKED THE PIERS of the marina. The sun was starting to hang low in the sky and the gulls cried and dove around them in pursuit of some schooling fish that had wandered too close in to the shoreline and become stranded in the receding tide.

Ginny had recently returned to her post at the marina, maintaining that Dub needed her there more than she was needed at the zoo. Hugo, who seemed to have a knack for it, had taken the responsibility of the zoo mostly upon himself and appeared to be enjoying it immensely. The aloof doctor had found that after his many years spent living as a nomad, having a permanent place and purpose within a community brought him real happiness, something that had eluded him for as long as he could remember. Men are, after all, not meant to be alone in the world, but one can forget that if they work hard enough to, and Hugo had to relearn what it meant to truly be alive and a part of something.

He cared for the animals with the attention and tenderness that one might employ in the care of a beloved family pet and, in a way reminiscent of Ginny's departed father, he took solace in the knowledge that he was now preserving life as opposed to taking it. Ginny and Blake, easily perceiving the positive effect that the zoo was having on him and determining not to deprive him of it, left him to run the place as he saw fit and never saw any reason to intervene.

As for the relationship between Ginny and Hugo, they became fast friends. The old jealousies of the doctor that had led to his initial rupture with Blake had long since burned out and, to their mutual delight, they would spend hours together in Blake's library poring over books and then discussing what they had read.

Ginny basked in Hugo's vast experience in very much the same way she had always basked in Blake's, and Hugo finally seemed to realise that Ginny's presence in the library did not mean that his had to be elsewhere. Blake, for his part, was beyond happy to see his friend getting on so well with the woman he loved, and would often join them himself and participate in their lively discussions.

Tonight, meandering down one of the marina's several piers, Blake and Ginny waited for Hugo, who was to join them for an evening stroll in order to discuss the zoo. They walked slowly amongst the moored boats in the harbour, occasionally watching as a gull made a mad dive towards the increasingly vulnerable school of fish that remained marooned by the emergence of low tide's first sandbar. They saw Dub's head pop out of the door to his waterfront office and waved at him. He gave them a quick wave in reply and then disappeared back through it. Blake and Ginny continued their slow amble until they came across the black and stately ship, bearing gold lettering that read: *Eugenia.* They stopped and looked up at it for a while. Just then they heard the familiar steps that announced the arrival of Hugo Wegener.

They turned to meet him as he said, "Lots to discuss, my friends! Lots to discuss."

Blake and Ginny smiled at him as he gave them an animated report on the current happenings at the beloved zoo. They were pleased to hear, but not surprised, that business was good and that the animals were happy. The high point of the doctor's account was the announcement that one of the zoo's residents was pregnant, and that the veterinarian had concluded, after a thorough examination, that everything looked just fine. This announcement gained greater eminence when they learned that the animal in question happened to belong to a particularly rare species, and that a birth such as the one they hoped for would likely bring their small operation some national attention.

Ginny leaned into Blake and listened contentedly as the doctor went on excitedly. His obvious passion for his life's new calling warmed both their hearts, and they always looked forward to his reports.

When Hugo had finally finished his recap, Ginny turned to Blake and said half-jokingly, "I don't think Hugo needs us anymore, Ainsley. Whatever are we going to do with ourselves?"

Blake looked down lovingly into Ginny's face and then back up to the *Eugenia*'s great black hull, and said, "You've always wanted to see the world. Maybe it's time for a trip?"

Ginny beamed at him and whispered, "Really?"

"Why not?" replied Blake simply.

Ginny looked thoughtful for a moment, then turned. Blake followed her gaze to Dub's office and understood.

Ginny thought for a long time, her eyes fixed on Dub's curtained window. Through it, she could just make out his face, bespectacled and hunched down close to some papers on his desk. As if sensing that he was being watched, he glanced up from his work and met Ginny's eyes. At that moment, Ginny knew that he would be alright. She knew that he would want her to go, to experience, as any father would. There was so much genuine tenderness in his eyes that her own began to shine with tears. Dub smiled at her and gave a slight nod, almost as if he understood the conflict she was facing in her heart and was determined to rid her of it.

The three friends stood at the water's edge and watched as the sun dipped slowly below the horizon. The sky was painted with warm streaks of orange, red and yellow. So much had happened since the arrival in town of the mysterious stranger, Ainsley Blake.

There had been pain, but there had been so much more than that too. There had been love – the only true love that Ginny Harrison had ever known. There had been friendship and loyalty. She had lost a father but gained a partner for all the rest of her life.

She knew in that moment, watching the sun disappear in a burst of soft orange glory, that she would go. That she would leave this place and likely never come back. Dub had given his blessing and, watching the darkening sky, she knew that her father had given his, too. She looked over at Hugo and knew that he would protect her father's dream, then she looked at Blake and knew that he would protect her heart. The young girl had triumphed over tragedy, and as the sun's last rays vanished into the sea, she felt them reborn inside herself and restored to their full brightness.

When Ainsley Blake again met the eyes of Virginia Harrison, he saw at last that which he had so been yearning to find in them. It was that bright fire that had always burned in her gaze, revealing a spirit both indomitable and delicate, kind but untamed. It was that light that so infected all of those who came into contact with her, and that had nearly been extinguished by the loss of her father. It burned now with even greater ferocity than it had at the peak of its former glory.

Blake drank it in and it excited him. When the sun had gone away completely, they looked up to the *Eugenia* and knew their path. No one spoke, but Blake's thoughts took him back many years to the handsome English estate house of the first Lord Blake. Gone for so many years but alive always in the present Blake's heart.

He thought about the promise he had made to the dying old man, and how he had decided long ago that it was to remain forever unfulfilled. He looked down at Ginny, her eyes like fire, and smiled. He had protected her. He would protect her still, and always. At long last, he would fulfil the promise he had made to his late father and return honour to the name of Blake.

It would not be the honour of dukes nor lords, but of ordinary people. The honour brought by righteous deeds and selfless actions. The honour of having the courage to love and then being true in service to that love. He knew that this had been the type of honour that his late father had intended all along. Blake looked beyond Ginny to his friend, and then up to the office window, where Dub could still be seen silhouetted against the curtain, poring over his papers. He looked back to Ginny and then out to the endless sea. For the first time in untold years, Ainsley Blake was happy.

-EPILOGUE-

H IS EYES OPENED, BUT HIS GAZE WAS UNFOCUSED. BROKEN light shone through the canopy of trees above him, but his eyes still needed time to adjust. He remembered that it had been dark before. His body ached all over, so he lay still, trying to gather his thoughts. Something had happened, but he couldn't remember exactly what. He racked his aching brain and closed his eyes hard as if to force a recollection, but nothing came. He opened them again and noticed that his vision had cleared. With effort he sat up, looking around himself. He was in the forest and everything seemed familiar to him. How he had ended up so far from where his people slept, however, he did not know. His vision blurred again but only briefly, then refocused. The pain in his head was so great that he felt as though it might split open. He put his hands to his temples in an attempt to push back on the immense pressure that seemed to be forcing itself outward from inside his brain. A cacophony of sounds reverberated around inside his skull, so loud that it sounded as though they were borne from within him as opposed to without. He could hear scurrying animals, the crunching of sticks and leaves and birds singing all around him, their volumes inexplicably amplified. The noises drowned out his own thoughts and confused him. In addition to the noise, there was the smell. Many smells, all on top of each other. They made his stomach turn. He could smell everything as if it were right under his nose. There was the forest, of course, but there were also far more unsettling smells intermingling with it. Foreign and alarming. He could smell blood, sweat, recently turned earth and the smoke of fires long burned out. He had seen the aftermath of tribal conflict before and this is what he smelled now. Somehow, despite this, all around him looked peaceful and undisturbed as if by enchantment. His vision stabilised now, returning in full force, and, in truth, he could not remember ever having seen so clearly. He followed the many sounds that were assaulting him to their sources, and found squirrels, birds and other tree-dwelling creatures so far up in the canopy that he felt as though it must be some trick of his mind that he was able to see things so impossibly small and far away, much less hear them.

He rose from the spot on which he had awoken, overwhelmed by the buzz of activity that attacked his senses, and turned in the direction of the scent that had alarmed him most. He began to make his way towards it and found that he had an added bounce in his step for which he had not accounted. It seemed that his whole body had become lighter, and so much so that each step he took threw him awkwardly off-balance. With some difficulty, he mastered the coordination of his new muscles and tread lightly, eventually finding his normal stride. He paused again after a few steps, finding himself unable to bear the continued assault on his senses. He closed his eyes and concentrated with such force that he felt the rogue perceptions beginning to bend to his will. They were not silenced, just focused, categorised, relegated to a back portion of his mind and persisting as a low hum that could be called again into focus through another force of will if needed. The smells, too, could be controlled, individualised or filed off to the side for consideration at some later time. He stood still as he worked through this internal maintenance process and, when he had finally regained control of himself completely, he reopened his new eyes and saw the majesty of the world through them for the first time in all its glory.

He resumed his course towards the terrifying smells of battle, worrying that their presence meant that some great misfortune had befallen his kinsman. He quickened his step and found that he could move with preternatural speed, blurring the trees as he wove through them with inhuman agility. In seconds, he found himself at the source of the ghastly odour. The devastation was absolute. Blood stained the forest floor, pooling in places as it raced away from the bodies from which it had sprung. He employed his supernatural hearing so as to locate any survivors, but found none. His eyes filled with tears as the realisation that he was alone began to dawn on him. Everyone whom he had loved, everyone with whom he and his loved ones had shared their simple lives, was gone. Their bodies lay spread throughout the modest camp, looking as though they had had no knowledge of an attack. They looked peaceful and, were it not for the blood that painted the whole of the camp, one might have assumed that they were asleep.

He tried to remember. What had attacked with such stealth, killed with such efficiency, that its victims were gone before ever knowing that they were threatened? A flash came back to him suddenly. Something dark had come. There had been a successful hunt and they had been feasting. He, however, had been off by himself and quite alone, resting, when the festive voices and rhythmic drumbeats had ceased all at once. He had peeked out from where he had been lying and that's when he had seen it. Seen something. It moved as a blur, impossible to behold with any clarity, spilling blood in its wake and letting the bodies fall indifferently to the forest floor. He had been frozen with fear and had been forced to witness, without moving a muscle, the slaughter of the whole of his people before he had finally snapped back to himself and run for safety.

The creature had been upon him in an instant but, when he was sure that death was about to take him, it relented, backing off and disappearing again into the trees. He had lain there for a long time, weak and dying, mourning the loss of his people and of his own life, which he was sure was slipping away from him. He wondered what it was that had been their destroyer. Some demon, not a man. Weighed down by the enormity of the loss, he welcomed death. But death never came, only rebirth.

He looked at the carnage through his inhuman eyes and smelled the destruction with his animal nose. He heard the chatter of far-off villages through ears that could hear all, and knew that his life had changed forever. He wondered, would it be a gift, or a curse? The only thing that was certain was that he had been reborn anew, and what he had been was gone forever. He thought about who he was supposed to be now that everything he was had been destroyed. And, though he would go on to assume countless aliases in the time that was to follow, it was still to be a great many years before he would come to be known by the honourable and lordly name of Ainsley Blake.